BLIZZARD

BLIZZARD

A NOVEL

MARIE VINGTRAS

TRANSLATED FROM THE FRENCH
BY JEFFREY ZUCKERMAN

THE OVERLOOK PRESS

Originally published in 2021 in France by Éditions de l'Olivier

Library of Congress Control Number: 2022946037

ISBN: 978-1-4197-6590-2
eISBN: 978-1-64700-895-6

Printed and bound in the United States

10 9 8 7 6 5 4 3 2 1

Abrams books are available at special discounts when purchased in quantity
for premiums and promotions as well as fundraising or educational use.
Special editions can also be created to specification. For details, contact
specialsales@abramsbooks.com or the address below.

ABRAMS The Art of Books
195 Broadway, New York, NY 10007
abramsbooks.com

To Elena and Arto

BLIZZARD

BESS

I lost him.

I let go of his hand to retie my laces and I lost him.

My foot was loose in my shoe, I wasn't about to waste time taking it off, and I couldn't be falling over now. Damn laces. I could have sworn I'd tied a double knot before leaving.

If Benedict were here, he'd have said I wasn't paying attention, he'd have been clear I wasn't doing things right, meaning his way. The only way, in his eyes. Oh, sure. He can think that all he likes, but there'll always be as many ways to do things as there's people on earth.

Never mind that: How long has it been since I let go of his hand? One minute? Two? When I stood up, he wasn't there anymore.

I swung my arms all around to try to grab him, I called his name, I yelled as loud as I could, but all I got back was the whistling wind. I already had a mouth full of snow and my head was spinning.

I lost him and I can't ever go back home. He wouldn't understand, he doesn't have all the facts. If he'd asked the right questions, if I'd answered him truthfully, he'd never have trusted me with the boy. He decided not to say a thing, keep up the charade, believe that I could do what he was asking me to do. And here all I'm doing is making things worse, adding to this hell.

As if I could help it.

BENEDICT

Come to think of it, I'd say I could tell something was off. A bit like when you get the feeling a bug's buzzing by your ear, maybe. You swat at it, but it turns out it's an alarm, the alarm in your head, quiet as can be. It won't make you jump, there's just enough to keep you from a good night's sleep, though.

So I didn't sleep much and I bolted awake. Did I have a feeling right then, or was it only the draft coming in from below? I couldn't guess. I was so tired after those days checking the traps, stowing equipment, and getting ready before the bad weather comes.

I've always been fond of storms—right before them, especially, when you've got to gear up for everything, seal all the gaps, haul in enough wood to last a few days, and hunker down as best as you can. And then, once the storm's come, I just curl up with the CB radio sputtering, a hot mug of coffee to warm my hands, and a fire kicking up a fuss, what with the snow and the wind coming down the chimney.

I hear the house groaning and shifting like an old man. Sometimes I get it in my head it's talking to me, the way it likely talked to my old folks and their own old folks before them, generations and generations all the way back to the very first Mayer who put down roots here, on land no tree could grow on, to prove that he knew something nature didn't.

The house's still standing and I'm nice and warm inside, like a diamond in a box. Problem is, I'm all alone.

When I came downstairs, the door was wide-open and the snow was already blowing in by the shovelful. I couldn't believe my eyes. I yelled out for Bess, asked her why she didn't shut the damn door, shouted that we'd all be dead of cold no thanks to her, but I got no answer. And then I saw the little boy's boots weren't there and that their jackets weren't hanging on the rack.

Then I knew she'd gone out with him, never mind that even a girl as different as her ought to know that you never go outside when the blizzard's at its worst.

COLE

You listening, God? I swear to you I'll never drink another drop. Whatever that bastard gave me is killing my head. "Rotgut" doesn't even begin to cover it. No feeling left in my throat, and my stomach's an unholy mess. That stuff will make a nun out of you, and I don't even have the getup for that.

I was barely out of the bathroom, no thanks to the shits from the booze, when I heard someone hammering at the door. No good Christian would be outside in weather of this sort, so I bundled myself up as best as I could and grabbed my gun. No telling what could be running around in those woods.

I hollered, "Who is it?" as if a bear could shout back, but there was too much wind out there to hear a thing. The pounding only got worse. Well, no choice now. I turned the lock, got the door open with my foot, and stuck the barrel through just in case.

"Don't you shoot, Cole. It's me."

Benedict. I'd know that deep, booming voice anywhere. He was covered in snow—it was on his shoulders like some two-bit general's epaulets—and he already had white-tipped eyelashes with bits of frost hanging off them like some stripper all done up. I'm only saying that because I saw a picture of one in a magazine at Clifford's. A pretty face with little drops at the ends of her big fake lashes that made her look like a silly life-size doll. Some men must like that.

Benedict shoved his way in and got the door shut behind him. Didn't even pull off his hat. He was leaning on the wall, running his hand over his face. Looked like he'd just seen a ghost.

"Bess and the kid are gone. They're out there."

Them? Out in the storm? The idea was so wild I let out a guffaw.

"Now, now, Benedict, that's an awful long way you've come just for a joke."

He shot back, "You think I'd go outside in this weather for a laugh?"

I took a good look at his face and I could tell he was dead serious. Well, damn. If it was true, then they really were in the shit. The kid's all of ten years old, that pip-squeak, and the woman wasn't the sharpest tool in the shed. So I asked him: "Well, what do you want me to do about it?"

I didn't like the sound of what he said next one bit: "What do you think? You and me are going to go find them."

That right there was worse than Clifford's hooch. It almost made me want to take another swig.

FREEMAN

I couldn't sleep a wink with this storm. The wind's blowing so hard around the house that I don't see how it's still standing. There's the gusts coming in on one side and the snow heaping up on the other that's got the walls in a vise. Lord knows how I'll make my way out when it's all past.

The first time I weathered a storm here, it was two days before I could get outside. There was a good five feet of snow in front of the door, and those window shutters I'd been foolish enough to shut weren't opening. "Rookie mistake," Benedict said later on. I might be an old man, but I still had to climb up to the attic and come down through the dormer with a rope. That wasn't easy going. I popped my shoulder out on the way down, and I still had to shovel snow with my good arm before I could find something to keep the other one where it belonged. This time I decided I'd clear as much as I could around the house, maybe that'd be enough.

Staying alive isn't something you can just figure out as you go. Where I come from, nobody has to wonder if snow's going to shut them in. There's no snow, not one flake, and if I had the choice, with these joints of mine, I'd sooner be there than in this place. The cold, the damp—that's no good for this old body. That'd really be something, to have lived through everything I did only to die now, rotting like a moldy old branch.

What am I doing here, anyhow? I reckon if He's bent on us meeting and on me being buried at the end of the world, then He has His reasons for it. He knows I'm a sinner, but if God in all His mercy has a plan for me, then I'll wait on the answers. I'm frozen, and I'll still wait as long as I have to. Lord knows, I don't have much say in the matter.

BESS

I don't see a thing. The snow's swirling all over the ground, and when I look up, the whole sky is full of specks. The air's got no color to it, like every single tint's gone, like all the world's been watered down.

I wish I'd listened when Benedict was trying to tell the kid how blizzards work. Maybe I'd have known what to do, other than not going out, but what's done is done.

I've got my back to the wind. I'm leaning against what I reckon's a rock. Unless it's a bear hibernating . . . Oh, that'd take care of things.

I can't even decide what to do next, but if I don't get a move on, I'll end up a snowman. I'm not as stupid as that. I know how much of a mess I'm in. I need to keep going, find the kid, or head home to get Benedict.

But if he sees that the kid's lost, he'll go right to pieces. I can't go back, I can't tell him what happened: that's too much. He's got both feet on the ground, but some things will knock even men like him for a loop. Anyway, I can't leave the kid all on his own.

Which way do I even go? Straight ahead, I guess. That's what he must have done. Kids can be stupid sometimes, do things without thinking, just by instinct, even a little genius like him. So if I don't think, I'll just walk straight ahead. That's got to be the best thing to do.

BENEDICT

Cole's taking his sweet time getting ready. He's dragging his feet.

Can't really blame him, though. Who'd want to go out in this weather? Living here's hard enough when there's no snow, but in the worst of a storm you're in the belly of the beast—that's what Freeman says. I didn't go by his place. He's too old and his eyes aren't that good. What he came here for, I can't even guess. I let out a guffaw when he showed up two years ago with his van and his brand-new gear. Like one of those retirees who comes up to have himself a good time.

Living here, though, in a quiet corner like this, all alone—that's not really something you hear about around these parts. And he's the only Black man for miles. He sticks out just as much as Bess did when she settled here in a miniskirt and those white cowboy boots of hers. For his age he's in better shape than those boozers Clifford or Cole ever would be, but still he didn't look one bit like a guy here to get a taste of the wild. I figured he wouldn't last the winter in his mittens and his beanie hat. He was always tight-lipped about what he'd done before coming here, apart from being drafted for Vietnam. Maybe that's how he stuck through the first winter.

We didn't help him then. Around here, we'll help out our fellow men, but we're not going out of our way for a stranger. I did lend him a hand the first time he had to change the drive belt on his snowmachine, though. He'd bought it off of Clifford, just as crooked as always. Some things it's wisest not to buy used here. If someone's getting rid of it, there's a good reason why. It broke down so many times that Freeman had to go through every page of the manual that Clifford gave him. He'd never taken it out of its shrink-wrap. Makes me wonder if he knew how to read. Freeman took the whole machine apart, and after he'd put it back together, it worked even better than my own—not that that's saying much. Anyone could see Clifford wasn't all too happy. That crook thought he'd pulled a fast one on Freeman by selling him a dud, but the joke was on him.

And that was when I finally saw that, for an old man, Freeman was awfully resourceful. When he banged up his shoulder, he turned up at my door, wasn't even moaning, just asked if I could take him to see a doctor because he couldn't drive on his own. I wasn't all that keen on driving a good fifty miles to the free clinic, but I took him anyway. He'd gotten through his first winter here; nature wasn't going to get one over on him. Maybe, in a way, it'd made its peace with him.

I can't say as much of Bess, or the kid. One day she said that it was a real laugh, the two of them around these parts. That was her way of saying what everyone was thinking: the two of them had no business being here. I don't know if nature's taken a liking to them or if it's going to spit them out alive or dead. All I know is it's my fault. I shouldn't have brought them here. I know I promised the kid's mother that I'd keep him with me, but I shouldn't have. And now I'm out in a blizzard, looking for a kid and a girl in the middle of nowhere.

COLE

One thing I'll say: I had no desire to go out there. Only an idiot would do that.

Sure, I wasn't hinting as much to Benedict, but odds are they're already frozen dead or at the bottom of one of those crevasses in the ground by the lake, or worse. It's been a long winter, and some of the animals out there have an awful lot of teeth.

I even let Clifford know over the CB radio and he said not his problem, not sticking his head outside in this weather. No surprise there, although I figured he wouldn't mind finding the girl, if not the kid. I tried my darndest to drag my feet. I rummaged around for my warmest socks and also those fancy little silk liners that old Magnus always told me to put on first, even if they'd been darned so many times that it was only by the grace of God they didn't fall apart. Course, we'd still end up frozen worse than Eskimos.

Benedict was waiting on me, leaning on the doorframe. He looked like he'd aged ten years in a split second. Knowing they were out there had to be the worst thing he could imagine, and he was one to know. Men caught in spring runoff, crushed flat by the tree they were chopping, found stiff like twigs in ditches—he'd seen more'n his fair share when he was little and the sawmill was still there. A kid and a pretty woman lost in a blizzard, though? Best as I can recollect, no such thing's happened before. And Benedict knew just why. 'Cause there's no sense in that, and everyone here's got some sense to them, because each thing you do costs you and Mother Nature never goes easy on you. That's the deal you get. You want to live here? Clean air, big game, plenty of fish? Full freedom, nobody to answer to, maybe not even a soul in sight for weeks on end? You can live here on your own, all on your own.

The day you find yourself face-to-face with a grizzly or your rig won't start when you're miles from your place, though, you got to accept that nobody's there to help you, nobody but yourself. That's not something that damn girl can get in her head.

I finally found those socks. I grabbed two dozen cartridges for the rifle. Benedict had his with him, too, and I was going to open the door when I remembered Clifford's hooch. Not a bad thing to bring on such a harebrained expedition, that. This way I won't even feel the worst of this mess.

BESS

It's a real struggle to keep moving no matter what, and I'm not sure it's getting me anywhere. There's moments, out here in the snow, when I could swear I saw something move, but the second I look again, it's gone. This damn snow won't just come straight down like nice, normal rain.

So I don't lose my head, I try to remember California, the beaches our parents took us to every Sunday after church, all four of us by the ocean, having sandwiches and playing cards and the sun making us sleepy.

I can't make myself feel that heat anymore. Around here, even in the summer, the sun doesn't even warm your bones. Just makes you think you're warm, but you're never actually warm. You never think you're baking in the sun.

Sometimes I dream about the Pacific: those long rolling waves, the salt on my skin, and the spray in my hair. All there is here is fresh water, gallons and gallons of it, lakes and rivers and streams and brooks and falls. Water, water everywhere, all the time: ice floes, snowmelt, crystal clear or muddy in the spring. And cold, always cold. Nothing you'd ever want to skinny-dip in.

I'd give anything to sunbathe on the beach again, listen to the waves crashing on the sand. It's funny: I can still remember the coconut smell of the sunscreen Mommy put on when I was little so she could tan and not burn her milky skin. She was so pretty back then, like a movie star. We weren't all that well-off, but she was always elegant. She was a small woman with the looks and the stomach of a fifties film star. Daddy was so in love with her that he said even Rita Hayworth didn't have anything on her. I didn't get what he was saying about some old actress who died the year I was born, but Mommy seemed to really like the sound of that.

Both Cassandra and he were blond, almost white-haired—that was the Scandinavian side showing. And I'd gotten Mommy's red hair, like a real Irish American. It was a burden, but everyone always knew who we were from a mile off. "Look who it is: that's Elizabeth Morgensen and her mother."

When I was a teen, I was so scared I'd end up a bad copy of her. I didn't have my boobs yet and my hips were as skinny as a boy's. I wasn't anything close to a sex symbol, not even an old one. Then her hair went gray overnight. She tied it in a long, faded braid and it was stained yellow at the end from nicotine. She was always dressing to be seen, and then, snap, she let herself go. Why hang on to bits of cloth or tubes of lipstick when what mattered most was gone?

I always did my best to forget the dead, and now I was trying to forget that side of her too. And then I gave up just like her, but in my own way. I guess all we had in common was our looks. But I still can't shake her.

The kid's out there, and Lord knows I've got to save him. I can't make the same mistake twice.

BENEDICT

We set off from Cole's and we moved about as fast as convicts in chains. By the clock it was still morning, but we couldn't even see the sky to be sure.

On my way to Cole's, I was wondering where they meant to go in this weather. It was always a mystery to me what those two were thinking. Did the kid forget something and want to go get it? He's always carrying around a book or that magnifying glass of Magnus's I gave him when we got here so he wouldn't be so unhappy living in this place. He's small for his age, but he's still like a little professor with his glasses and his books under his arm. He was only four when he learned how to read and write, and then six years old when he was doing math in his head. And then there's Cole, who can't even add two and two. When that boy talks to me, I feel stupid. Ma tried to teach us things, but I could never keep up. This little guy actually puts you to shame. And I know he doesn't mean to; he's not out to make people feel bad about themselves. He just is who he is, nothing more. He's "got potential," like his mother used to say. And I was the one she told about that "potential," like I had any way of helping him there. She said, "Benedict, promise me you'll take care of him," and all I could get out was that it wasn't right to ask that kind of thing of me, that I could barely breathe in this city where I couldn't stretch my arms without hitting someone, where people's hearts were colder than any heart you'd find here in Alaska. I told her, "Don't ask me to stay here: that'll be the death of me," and she said, "Benedict, take him anywhere you like, but promise me you'll keep him close. Don't ever let him wander off."

And what did I do? I brought him here and I let him get lost. I didn't even watch him like I'd promised to. I didn't teach him what Pa taught me. I didn't pass on what any father was supposed to pass on to his son.

FREEMAN

She wrote to me again. She's always writing me letters, like we're in some other century. I won't say it suits me— my eyes are getting bad and I could do with some new glasses—but she won't do things any other way, not that there's all that many other ways hereabouts. No Internet, and the satellite phone's spotty. So she writes. A letter a week, sometimes more, sometimes less. Sometimes it's just a few words, sometimes it's pages and pages where she's going on and on about her instructions, as if I didn't already have them down cold from when I was there.

Picking up her letters means going all the way to the post office, although I don't go every week now. I don't see the point. At first, there were things to tell her about, and that seemed to keep her happy. But now she's just getting older and getting needier. She thinks I'm not telling her enough.

What I wouldn't give to see her here, show her that it's nature that sets the pace and that means things move slowly, very slowly. Winter months where nothing happens, where you just while away the hours reading or fixing up odds and ends around the house, and summer months—if you could call it summer—where the real work happens, and there's so much to tend to even though I'm getting on in years.

I know how to wait. I've spent years on the lookout, waiting here is nothing new for me. Sometimes, though, it feels like I'm starting to disappear. I've lost too much time hoping for something to shift, watching for the signs, and now I'm at that age where time's a precious thing I haven't got so much of anymore. Here, you can forget everything and be forgotten. Now that I've probably given her the answers she wanted, I do hope she remembers she's the one who sent me to this corner of the world. I won't be around forever. I'm too old now.

COLE

We've already been walking a long while. Benedict was dead set on snowshoes, not the machine. Said we couldn't have followed any tracks if we'd even found any, and we'd have ended up in a crevasse in no time.

I've got my big headlamp and spare batteries, keeping them warm in a sock tied to my belt, seeing as the cold would just drain them. It was old Magnus who taught me that trick. I didn't know the first thing when I started living in these parts, but he taught me everything—did it with the patience of a saint, as if that could make up for lost time. He taught me how to set traps, pick up the lines, and do the dirty work: gut animals, scrape the skins to remove the meat. He also taught me how to recognize animal tracks, figure out which ones were prey animals and which ones *we* were the prey for. My own father never taught me none of that, all he was good for was giving me a hiding every time I was in his way so I'd regret being alive. Magnus showed me everything and never once asked me what had brought me up here. I don't think he ever asked anyone what'd brought them to his doorstep.

He also taught me always to leave a light on in the house before going, and so I did, just like Benedict. A light in the night, or in the blizzard, for when you're lost. Like a lighthouse in a storm. Means there's a human being somewhere and maybe you'll get through the worst of it.

We followed the path as best as we could from Benedict's rather than following the road. He was saying we had to put ourselves in the boy's shoes, but who knows if it wasn't the woman taking the lead. She's not all there, she could have gone any which way, maybe she even went home, back Outside.

There's no making someone from the Lower 48 love it here. I don't get why he brought her up. I figured him for a sourdough with his head screwed on right, not one of those city slickers who gets all turned around on our roads every summer so they can "commune with nature" with their big ugly glasses and GPS devices that don't work and pants rolled up like they're going fishing and like there isn't a single mosquito around.

You live here, you don't dress for looks. You dress so you won't freeze your balls off and so you won't get your toes frostbitten and have to cut them off. Sometimes that still happens no matter how careful you are, like Moses, who's only got one toe now on his left foot, or Hanson the Swede—not that he's got all that much to do with Sweden nowadays—who's missing two fingers thanks to his chain saw slipping out of his hands. That'd never happen to me, though. I've got my wits about me. In normal weather, at least, when I'm not outside looking for a kid and a madwoman. That's no fault of mine. It's all hers, and more than that it's Benedict's fault. Just going by how he's walking, though, bent double, that sad sack knows it already.

BESS

None of them, not even Benedict, thinks I have my head on straight, I know it. Sometimes I'll hear them snicker when I walk out of a room or when I go up to bed. I'll hear Cole talking about me, Benedict not saying a word, and I always grab the stair railing as hard as I can to keep me steady, I clutch until my knuckles go white.

I know I look crazy, but I wasn't always like that. When I was little, I had just one screw loose. Daddy was always telling me that was what made me special. He called it my best feature, because that way nobody'd ever forget me.

After we lost Cassandra, though, I didn't react the way I was supposed to. I didn't know what we were supposed to do at times like that. I figure nobody does. There's no how-to book to tell you what to say, what look to give people, what other folks expect of you. I knew I was getting odd stares because I wouldn't change, not even on the day of her funeral. I was wearing my yellow T-shirt, the one with Jim Morrison in a blond wig, that was the one she'd liked best, the one I'd never let her borrow. I'd have given anything for my sister to be able to ask me for it, for me to be able to tell her she could have this shirt and anything else she asked for. That's why I wore it that day and not black clothes. That would have been anything but paying my respects.

Nobody understood. Nobody understood that part of me was missing, that there was a hole in my body and all the air I breathed in went out it. I didn't know how to cope, so I acted like nothing mattered. Only a fool would think that, but they were all fools. Sometimes grown-ups really are that blind.

I don't think I'm actually crazy, at least no more than those guys who got it in their heads that it would be nice to up and move to this hell. That creep Cole, who thinks he's as sly as a fox but who's good and stuck here. Anyone can see he couldn't hack it in the city, since that's a whole different ball game. Clifford's not a talker but I've seen how he always looks at me, it'll make your blood run cold, like living here's made an animal out of him. And Freeman— I don't even know his first name—he's decided to retire here, never mind that he doesn't have the muscles or the brains of any of the others. I don't get it. Nature, wide-open space—maybe those are magic words that change everything. Wide-open space, ah, there's no lack of that in the world, and you won't get half as bored elsewhere.

Myself, I've always liked it when there were people all around. I never feel lost when I'm in a big crowd, it's like being in a school of fish. I always watched them go by and wondered if the man who killed her was there, with all the others, his Lakers cap covering his eyes. Maybe he's just like me, looking at the bodies all around to pick out a face. Except he'd be out for some little thing to snatch, a little, light, fragile thing he could just grab and break in two.

BENEDICT

It's the details I got to watch for—some bit of cloth, or a toy in the snow, or a twig snapped clean, or a dip in the ground here—but the blizzard means I can't see much. Sometimes, all of a sudden, the wind stops. Everything floats down like pillow feathers and I can just about pick out what's all around, but it's always here one second and gone the next.

Pa used to say that was worse than the storm proper: right when everything's still, like when you're in the eye of a hurricane, and you start to get a bit hopeful, but it goes by just like that, and then you're in the thick of it again. Hunched and cursing about being so bundled up, you're sweating in your parka. That damn sweat will give you chills or make you thirsty enough to want to stuff some snow in your mouth.

The times I can see more than ten feet ahead, I cross my fingers that I can pick out the boy's shape and Bess's too.

Looking proud, sticking out her chin like she wants to be taller than she is. That's what really throws men for a loop, that feeling she gives off that nobody can touch her. She's awful pretty with her light skin and her red hair, sure, but she's a wild card too. I have no idea what's going on in her head. I still figured it would be a good idea, her being better educated than anyone here, not that that's saying much, and she wanted to get the heck out of Dodge. I needed someone for the kid, someone to teach him things, but of course it wasn't long before she was out of her element too. Thing is, he's learned plenty from books but just about nothing when it comes to staying alive around these parts. What does it matter if you know every last thing about that plate-tectonic stuff if you don't know what to do when you get hit by a quake? He can tell me the names of every single ocean trench in the world, but he can't even land a minnow, never mind gut and cook the fish. Cole said he'd make a man out of the boy. Teach him all "Magnus's rules for staying alive" in the spring. Just that, though—for school stuff he's the last one who could help, even if he's a city man from Outside and has no excuse.

I can't watch over him here forever. He needs to be schooled, just like any kid his age, and she's going to be trying her damndest to get him back again. Christ, what good am I for a kid in such a godforsaken corner? What can I show him but these views and snow, more snow than anyone's ever seen?

FREEMAN

I'm not the sort to complain. God put me here. I'm trying to convince myself that it's He who set me on my way even as I've erred.

Martha used to say that even the worst sinners can witness a miracle. I won't say a miracle, but I've come to think that helping her has to be some form of salvation. Not forgiveness for what I've done, but if the Lord saw fit for her to be the only one to see me, maybe He really does work in mysterious ways.

When I saw Magic's body with that red starburst spreading across his stomach, I was sure it was a mistake, that I was dreaming, that he was wearing one of those fake Hawaiian shirts with bright colors tourists love so much. But I was still holding that warm Beretta I knew so well tight in my hand. I wasn't set on him dying. How could I be?

I was sobbing like a fool when I saw her come out of the trees. She looked like a ghost with her white dress and her shiny silver belt, her gray hair parted ever so nice and coming down to her shoulders and her eyes that were so light blue they almost looked washed-out. They made her look like she wasn't even human. Truth be told, she terrified me. I figured she was an apparition and I could feel my whole body pulling back, like my heart would just snuff it in my rib cage, like I was going to fall apart, crumple up like a burst balloon. She looked at Magic on the ground with that starburst, which was a lake now, and the blood turning his whole shirt red. She glanced at him like he was just any old thing that'd fallen to the ground. She turned to me, eyed my hand still holding the gun like it wasn't nothing.

And when she looked me in the eyes next, she didn't seem scared. I couldn't tell you what she saw in this old man in a suit holding a Beretta over a body, but I think I recall the faintest bit of a smile on her face. She didn't give me a grin. It was a smile at something nobody but her could make out.

Later on, she proposed me a pact. Not with the devil, like I figured at first. A pact with God, she said. I didn't see how she might be in any position to do such a thing, but she was offering me a salvation of sorts if I could prove myself worthy. So, God, answer me this: Why would a white woman be there in Central Park so late in the evening, with no witness other than those ice-blue eyes of hers, if it wasn't a sign on Your part?

And all this while, every time I wake up, I can still see Magic standing over me. He doesn't say a thing, he's pale, he's laid his hand on that hole in his belly like he's ashamed of it, like he wants to hide it. And I, all I can do is curse myself for letting this rage that isn't like me get the better of me. All I can do is cry my eyes out for my son.

BENEDICT

The fresh powder's halfway up my thighs. Every step is a real struggle. Every step is a burn.

But that's nothing new. It was like that for us when we were kids with Pa out checking the traps or hunting and got caught in heavier snow than there was supposed to be. Pa had a sixth sense for the weather and it didn't often steer him wrong. If we weren't too far away, he got us home safe and sound so Ma wouldn't worry, otherwise he made us a makeshift shelter. I never saw him worry.

I don't think there was a single crevasse, cave, or knocked-over tree that he didn't know about. It was like he'd actually drawn the landscape himself, decided on the valleys, the hills, and the way every bit of water would go. If Ma heard me say that, she'd have called it blasphemy. You don't joke when it comes to the Lord. But all my childhood I kept thinking that Pa had created everything and that no other human being could know what he knew. When I asked him how he knew everything about every-thing, he just smiled. He said he didn't even come close to knowing everything, but what mattered most, aside from just going and seeing for himself, was trusting his instinct for getting out of tricky spots. He was convinced that nothing was smarter than our lizard brains—that you'd do well to listen to nature and listen to your gut. Pay enough attention, that'll show you everything you need—just the way the wind's shifted or how the birds stopped chirping.

Faye was tickled when I told her that. She said that in New York her friends paid a fortune for classes meant to help them "find" their "wild selves." Here, though? You find your wild self fast or you're dead. Thomas said maybe this was one of the last places where nature could still fight back, even after so much logging and offshore drilling, and what with the glaciers disappearing. There's no difference between now and a hundred years ago, only a few tiny details.

I wonder what Pa would have done if he were here, how he would have gone about trying to find the boy. But he never lost us outside to begin with. That wasn't a problem he ever had to deal with. He was too smart to make that kind of mistake.

COLE

Pity Benedict didn't ask the Black guy to come. Man's old
enough that with a bad fall that'd be two birds with one
stone. I was hoping he'd snuff it the first winter, I even said
it out loud to Clifford. Couldn't tell you why that guy was
so sure having been in the Army meant he'd hang in there.
But, sure enough, he's still alive. A stubborn fellow who'll
outlive everything like scorpions and cockroaches. They
say roaches can survive nuclear blasts. I wouldn't put it
past those Blacks either.

Sully's wife rented him the house. She had to after the
accident. She didn't have the money for the hospital bills,
so she had to rent out that shack at the end of the world,
a shack Sully'd built all on his own to boot.

Clifford told me she was sleeping at a motel by the
hospital and she was a house cleaner to pay off the

medical bills, but since she didn't have insurance, that wasn't enough.

That Lois was a respectable lady and she had to open up her house to a Black. He laid a whole wad of dollars down on the table and she couldn't say no because renters were plenty scarce around these parts. Sully hadn't done much upkeep for the place, not even with a woman living there.

Have to say, not many women would sign up to live here in the first place, keep house, fix the odd thing that broke, look after their man. Just women who'd put up with bare-bones living because they were too old for kids and pinching themselves that a man'd look twice at them.

Benedict's girl's a different story, though. Clifford and I couldn't believe our eyes when we saw her in a bathing suit the first summer like she was at the beach. It wasn't even all that warm. He said that it was the wildest sight, a body that wasn't all wrinkles and sagging skin, a thin body, with all the parts where they belonged.

You come here with a woman like that in tow, everybody'll be jealous of you. You're practically asking for trouble, and I don't think Benedict had the faintest clue. Maybe it occurred to him for half a second.

I'm not the only one who's found her awful easy on the eyes, and Magnus isn't there to protect him anymore.

BESS

I fell. I must have tripped on a stump and then I was rolling downhill like a snowball. At the bottom, I didn't even know which way was up. All I could feel was how much my ankle hurt and I was missing a shoe.

I've got a real knack for getting myself into the shit. This time it's not Cole saying it, it's me.

Daddy took me to a building site once. I was just ten or eleven, and he looked so proud to be showing off his oldest girl to his team. The guys all played along, joking around with me like I was one of them. I was walking around with my safety helmet on my head, acting like a big deal, and then I went and put my foot down on the edge of a tray of cement. It went everywhere—on the ground, all over my shoe. Daddy looked at me, let out a sigh, picked me up, set me on a low wall to pull off my shoe and wash it while the other workers cleaned up the mess.

He didn't even scold me, he never did. All he did was say, "Elizabeth, won't you stop acting like a big deal once in a while, just to let me get a breather?" and then he squeezed my nose and gave it a bit of a twist. "What ever am I going to do with you?"

I said, "I don't know, Daddy. What?"

And, just like always, he rattled off a whole list of the wildest things I could imagine.

When we got back home, Mommy was furious. She didn't think he'd been sharp enough with me, that he was letting me become a bad girl, that I wasn't being raised right.

Of course I liked him better. It was only once I was grown up that I realized he'd let her play bad cop. Nobody likes the one laying down the law. Maybe that's another reason he left: because he couldn't play it cool all the time anymore. He'd run out of reasons to be happy and balance out his wife's bad mood. He never told me off: he always said it wasn't my fault, that I shouldn't feel bad, but he must not have believed it enough to stay with us. He'd been in love with a strong woman who made all the decisions, and all she was now was bitterness, there wasn't anything there left to keep a house.

I groped around for my shoe and, by sheer luck, it was in arm's reach. I shook out the snow that had gotten in and pulled it on. The pain made me gasp. I must have sprained my ankle when I fell. But there was no point stopping, no use crying. I knew I had to save my tears for when the real hurt came.

BENEDICT

I'm still on autopilot. All I want is to see the shape of the kid, see him turn and look at me with that serious face full of questions. Some days we don't say a word, there's so much quiet between us that I can't speak.

I'm not a talker. Our pa always said that I was a doer and that Thomas did all the talking. But then Thomas up and went and left us scrambling through a whole mess even though we had everything we could need to make us happy for a hundred years to come.

Once, when we were kids, Thomas woke me up before there was any hint of dawn, he clapped a hand over my mouth and just whispered "Come!" and he wouldn't take no for an answer. I got out of my warm bed and pulled on my clothes fast to follow him as quiet as possible down a set of stairs we knew down to the last inch. We put our feet down in the right spots so a creak wouldn't wake Pa up. We were like hunters on the lookout, we snuck out of the house, went past the other homes where folks were still asleep, all the way to the bit of forest that hadn't been chopped down yet and around the lake to get as close as we could to the crevasses, that forbidden spot. Back when I was little, I thought the Earth had to stop flat to send birds flying off into the air, and I thought that was the perfect spot for birds to take off.

Thomas got on top of the last rock sticking out of the ground, puffed up his chest, put his arms out like he was the king of a world that would go on and on. He looked up and yelled like a warrior: "I'm Thomas, son of Magnus! Here's my brother, Benedict, young but brave! Together we'll win every battle!"

I was shivering, and my feet were hurting from all the pebbles poking through my slippers, but I looked at the only brother I had, who was so sure about our future that I didn't worry one bit about it, and I pounded my chest with my little fist, yelled as loud as I could: "Every battle! Hear, hear!"

Right there and then I was sure no frontier could stop us, no obstacle could hold us back.

I've never woken up the boy in the wee hours. I've never taken him with me and told him that he'll be the king of the world, the way his namesake did once. I don't believe fairy-tale stuff like that, now that I know the sorts of things the real world's got in store for us.

COLE

A good hour now we've been walking, if you can call it walking. Being outside in this weather—now, I don't recommend that. I didn't ask for any of this. Honestly, she could die for all I care. I'm not risking my skin for a pretty girl who's got no business being here.

I don't know what got into Benedict's head if it wasn't her sweet little ass. I didn't figure him for that sort, actually. With a mother like his, he had to know that she was no girl to take home. That lady, though, she knew what made for a good wife, someone who's there for her husband and doesn't give him trouble.

The worst part is I don't think they even sleep together. Clifford says they don't. He could tell from how they acted and he said she wouldn't be half so hysterical if she had a real man to give her what she needs.

I do wonder what the story is, though. Bringing a nice woman who isn't even that kid's mother here, putting her up in his place, in his parents' own bedroom, God knows why, and having her teach the kid from schoolbooks when he'd do better to learn how to use a rifle. He's a *Mayer*, not some fancy-schmancy East Coast boy. I told Benedict I'd show the boy the particulars of hunting and trapping and he said fine. He said maybe it'd be easier if it wasn't him who did it.

As soon as this blizzard's over and we get some sight of spring, I'll take him camping, no matter what that woman says. She doesn't want me to have anything to do with him—she said she wasn't letting him out of her sight—but Benedict wouldn't have any of her blather. Good on him. Look how good that lady was at not letting him out of her sight! Took him outside with her, and now see what Benedict gets for trusting the last Mayer around these parts to a pretty girl like that.

BESS

I don't have it in me to walk anymore, my legs are heavy and the wind's so harsh I want to give up. Feeling scared that something could have happened to him ought to keep me going, wanting to find him ought to give me the energy I need, but all I want is to lie down and sleep.

I ought to be dead of shame. Mommy used to say that only blameless souls have any right to sleep, and she always added that sinners die in pain and suffering. Did she still think that when it came to Cassandra, since she didn't live long enough to be a real sinner? Of course, I wasn't going to ask her that.

The wind's not so strong over by the trees. When I stopped to catch my breath, I squinted. Between two gusts, I thought I could make out the trees in that weird line like a wave south and east of the lake. Up to the north, the only thing around Clifford's house is rocks. No surprise that old creep should have a place in the toughest spot.

The boy says that the way the trees are lined up, they look like a green wave nature had to make to hold off the elements. If I'm seeing all this, maybe he did too. Maybe he's remembered that Thomas's house is at the end, safe under trees, and maybe the only shelter to be found around here. Maybe he's managed to get in and he's just waiting for me or sleeping. Or reading the book he's got to have stuffed between his coat and his fleece. Maybe we can huddle up and stay warm together while we wait for the blizzard to die down. Maybe I can at least explain what I can to him and then, once the storm's not so bad, we'll walk back home, looking all proud, to find Benedict, who won't even be mad at us. Maybe he'll actually be happy that we made it through so well and Cole himself will shut that mouth of his for once. And maybe I won't feel so shitty, I'll have done him proud.

But there's another thing Mommy liked to say: You can make a whole world out of maybes.

Things usually don't turn out the way I'd hoped.

FREEMAN

My life took a turn when I was drafted for Vietnam. It was exactly my sort who got sent there, my sisters were saying: too poor to say no, too stupid to fight it.

What they couldn't get into their heads was that it didn't bother me. I had no plans to be a draft dodger and I wouldn't have known how to anyhow. Anything that would make a man of me so I wouldn't stay the youngest boy in a family of girls was fine by me. It was in my nature to be calm and quiet, but leaving was a dream I clung to, even if that meant going to war.

Of course, I didn't have the first idea what being a soldier really was like. The image I had in my head was a far cry from any violence. Just look at a picture of me at nineteen, all smiles, a man who'd only just stopped being a child. No idea what lay ahead. Not that anyone at home knew much more than I did, but what my sisters couldn't make heads or tails of was how excited I was.

Not even boot camp got me down. I gave it my all, even if I wasn't cut out for any of it yet. I crawled in the mud, walked miles and miles with my feet bleeding in my boots, assembled and disassembled my M14 over and over while my instructor yelled in my face that I wasn't good for shit. I paid him no mind: I was sure I was just as American as anyone else, even if the others said I really was born yesterday and even if, in or out of my uniform, the higher-ups were never going to see me as anything more than a Negro.

I didn't put up a fight when I was assigned to the MOS everyone prayed not to get assigned to: infantry, meaning I was on the front lines as cannon fodder.

My bunkmate tapped me on the shoulder and told me that I'd be wise to get laid so I didn't die a virgin. I did like that fellow and he looked so serious that it almost broke my heart. He eyed me like a man headed for the gallows, and it was only then that I saw I hadn't really lived, that I hadn't had even one girl, that I'd be going so far away that my sisters wouldn't be able to find me on a map and I didn't even know for sure why that country in particular.

Was I scared? That I was. Did I feel any regret? Not really. I reckoned that God would be with me every step, because that was how I'd been raised, and I set off with the others for Louisiana and Tigerland, Fort Polk, for infantry training, then I was sent straight to Vietnam with no real idea whether I'd come back to America standing on my own two feet or in a thousand pieces in a sealed coffin.

For a long time I suspected that, if I hadn't gone, Leslie wouldn't have been so hung up on guns, on my uniform, wouldn't have been hell-bent on one of his own. Maybe, if I hadn't gone to 'Nam, he'd still be alive, still with me telling me stories about the girls batting their eyes at him at school, and I wouldn't be here, freezing to death, alone with my ghosts.

BESS

Cole can call me a stupid city slicker all he likes, but I'm no fool.

At the edge of the woods the pines are tight together, like they're trying to huddle up against the wind and the snow. I bumbled through, tree by tree, sticking out my arms to get my hand on the next trunk. It did me good to feel that rough surface through my gloves. There was something still standing in the middle of this blizzard.

It was so cold that somehow my ankle wasn't even hurting anymore. I couldn't tie my laces right and the snow was getting into my shoe with each step. I kept going at my own pace, groping forward, it's not like anyone else was moving fast in this weather. When I couldn't find any more trees to hold on to, I figured that I was there, that the house shouldn't be far off—and, sure enough, between two gusts, there it was.

All I could see was a brownish shape, but I'd know that steep roof anywhere. If I've been going the right way and if the boy's ahead of me, he's got to have seen it too. And he must have, he's obsessed with his uncle Thomas. He thinks that it's impossible to disappear without a trace these days. Oh, if only! Anyone can just go poof if they really want to, and I'm one to know. That's something that boy doesn't get. He's too logical—it'd never occur to him—and I guess that's some comfort to him, that someone would find us if we disappeared.

I do hope he's right and that Benedict's going to find us, even if he's probably looking for the boy, not me. He'd never say it, but I know he does love his kid. Sometimes I catch him looking at the boy like he's the golden calf, and there's real love in his eyes—and head-scratching too. The boy looks like him, but not really. He's picked up the man's tics, wrinkling his nose at tricky things. When they get frustrated, they just about bury their heads in their shoulders like two turtles. But otherwise their hair and eyes and so on aren't even close to the same. The little kid's taken after his mother plenty.

They don't talk much. Benedict doesn't know how to act around children, this is probably the first one he's taken care of. He's not in the habit of stringing three words together, while that idiot Cole's always jabbering at him about the weather or bears or the traps he's set or fish in the spring, the huge char he caught the very first time he'd cast his line with Magnus watching. And it's not Cole the kid needs to be hearing, it's Benedict. Who barely says a thing. Apart from Cole, it's me he talks to the most, but only to ask me for something he needs, a book or some paper, something he'd like to eat, like those damn boxes of Apple Jacks that Benedict gets at Roy's, a thirty-mile drive away. Roy puts in a special order for us every year. Fifty boxes in one go and Benedict does his best to keep them dry and safe from rats.

Now, that's a real picture, that guy built like a brick shithouse, carrying packages off the truck like they're fine china and going to all these lengths just so the kid can have a bit of his old life.

Of course, the boy can't stand the cereal anymore, but he doesn't want to say so and break Benedict's heart. Now, that's a childish thought: worrying about breaking someone's heart.

BENEDICT

He'd been gone for a year when Pa said it had gone on long enough. It wasn't like before: I think he was scared he'd never see his son again. And Ma wasn't much better. She couldn't sleep, she kept saying that one day she'd end up forgetting her own son's face, and she couldn't stand the thought. It was worlds apart from when we were young, when I was sure we'd be happy forever. Everything felt wobbly, like a leg was missing.

He'd snuck out like a burglar, no explanations, and now we were all off-kilter. I couldn't see why Thomas would do that to us, and even now I don't know why he'd do such a thing. Shut the door of his house, get into his car, and disappear.

A year before Pa decided he couldn't take it anymore, I'd gone to Thomas's because it'd been five days since we'd seen each other last. The house was empty. He'd taken a few clothes and his backpack, and I saw his copy of *Walden* wasn't on his chair by the fireplace anymore. I knew if he took his favorite book with him, that meant he was set on being away awhile. He could have gone on one of those solo hikes he was in the habit of taking, but something about the state he'd left the house in had me convinced he hadn't. His wood chisel and his other wood-carving tools were on the ground, in front of the hearth. And his wood-carved animals, too: he'd put a grizzly, a wolf, an elk, and a sea eagle in a half circle, like they were there to talk to me, but the house stayed quiet. I don't know why, but I got the feeling he wasn't coming back.

If he was going to say goodbye to everything around him, this nature he said he loved more than human beings, he had to have a damn good reason. But, that day, all I felt was angry at him, and it only got worse as our parents got worried and panicky.

It's so selfish to just leave without thinking about our feelings, like we wouldn't worry ourselves sick, like we'd just go on without him. I could have punched him for what he'd done to Ma and Pa, for the grief he put them through all the way to the end. Staying angry at him was what kept me going. It drove me to go looking for him down in the Lower 48, from the West Coast all the way to the East, no matter what I might find. I crossed the United States looking for him, and I didn't find any answers to the questions I kept asking.

COLE

I hollered at Benedict that we had to go back—no point to this, we were just going in circles—but it's like he didn't hear me. Probably couldn't what with all this wind. I tried to grab his jacket to get his attention, but I just fell face-first into the snow. Goddammit. I got up as best as I could, and Benedict hadn't seen a thing.

I could feel my temper coming on. I loaded my gun. I sure felt tempted to aim it at his ass so he'd think twice about dragging me outside in this kind of weather, but I didn't.

I shot the one round in the air. He jolted and turned around with a wild look. He must have thought there was an animal. Like there's any animal as stupid as us, going out in a blizzard.

I made it clear with my hands that we had to stop, that we needed to go back before things got worse, but he stayed put, well, as put as anyone can stay when the wind's blowing this hard.

Benedict waved back at me—that was his way of saying I could go home if I wanted—and then he turned back around and kept on going God knows where.

Old Magnus would have understood that there was no use. But I can't make heads or tails of Benedict, maybe because I don't have kids. Seeing him grow up with his brother, that was kids enough for me. Sully's son too. I was the one who brought what was left of his body to his father. Sometimes bears don't turn up their nose at a bit of man meat, especially when the man tried to shoot you down.

Maybe I'll end up having to take another body to another father. Not hers, though. She can rot right where she is.

FREEMAN

I survived Vietnam and I'm still hard-pressed these days to say how. I was there for three years and I'd have come back tall and proud if, a month before my deployment ended, I hadn't caught some filthy illness.

Now, that's a real laugh: it wasn't the fighting that got me, it was a virus. Almost three years without so much as a scratch, not a single bullet or machete blow or grenade explosion. I near regretted it once I was back in the States because nobody could believe I'd been through 'Nam. I must not have looked lost the way the other guys did. My body was different, though. I wasn't any heavier, just more solid, more sure of myself. Life had made a man out of me.

I couldn't tell you what saved my life back there. I wasn't the smartest one, or the strongest, or the cleverest. I was anything *but* that. All I know is I must have gotten every ounce of luck my unit had to its name. I took some pride in that at first. No matter where I went, I'd come back safe, I was some sort of perfect American soldier nothing could hit. After a few months, the others put two and two together: however bad the fighting got, bullets never hit me. Some guys thought I could be their lucky charm. They figured it was smart to stay close to me, but they figured wrong. They only fell even faster, like all the bullets that couldn't touch me went through them instead. Some guys reckoned as much as I did that it was a miracle; others just hated me. When you find yourself picking bits of bone off of your flak jacket and you know that's all that's left of the head of the guy who was right beside you, the guy you shared everything with—meals, fears, stories about girls back home—you've got every reason to be mad at the scrawny Black guy from nowhere who survives everything when nobody else is as lucky.

Top brass sent me out on recon so many times, hoping I'd come back hurt or maybe not come back at all, but it only stopped scaring me. I was playing with fire because I couldn't believe it myself either. There were times I even hoped I'd die or be hit bad, because there was something unholy about being the only man who hadn't suffered a thing in the middle of hell.

When I came back, the pastor said that the hand of God had been with me and that he had protected me as I was an innocent soul. That had me seeing red. There's no godly or earthly explanation for horror. The other men had no better reason than I did to die with their eyes open in a riverbed, with no shroud but leaves torn up by bullets.

BESS

The last steps were the worst. My head was hurting so bad, I pulled back my hood and right away I wished I hadn't. The sweat on my forehead froze the second the wind touched it. When I wanted to pull the hood back up, my fingers wouldn't move anymore.

I thought I'd never reach the house. Cole said it was haunted just to scare the kid, but I know there's nothing wrong with it. I go by it as often as I can, but I never tell Benedict. He won't take us there, he won't even talk about it. He's made a holy shrine or a cursed place of it, something like that. But it's not a crypt, it's just a house. A house asleep. It's no different from the day he left, with the dishes put away above the sink, the bed made. There's nothing lying around. The books he read as a kid are on a shelf in his bedroom beside a family photo, the only one

I've ever seen since I got here. Magnus and Maud standing behind their two sons, with the glowing faces of people who have it all. The two boys sitting side by side with the same plaid shirt that their mother must have sewn them. Benedict almost a carbon copy of his father, Thomas taking after his mother down to her almond eyes and her complexion, which stands out even in a faded photo. He could have been a girl with his crossed legs and his long, thin fingers resting ever so carefully on his thighs, while his brother's got his arms crossed over his chest, the palms of his hands tight under his armpits, a bit of swagger there even though he can't have even been ten yet.

Besides that sole proof of an era that's totally gone now there are some toys, probably handmade by his pa and with the paint peeling off over time, a little round wooden box with baby teeth, and another with a glass lid holding a lock of blond baby hair tied off with a ribbon. Who'd have thought a man could be so sentimental? Maybe he didn't even know that he was leaving for good when he walked out of his house. Maybe he thought he'd be back soon. Benedict said that it had been too long now for him to ever come back.

At first, I thought that maybe he wasn't actually gone— that he might have had a bad fall and that his body was buried somewhere, under rocks that slipped under him, pine needles getting into the folds of his clothes. But Benedict said that he'd left the Interior, that some cousins had seen him at the Anchorage airport. His car was in the parking lot. He must have taken a plane somewhere.

Benedict never told me where. Why should he? I'd never met Thomas, after all.

But I know something about him that his own brother doesn't. Since I came here whenever I needed an escape, I'd gone through everything: closets, drawers, jars. I looked under rugs, linens, anything I could lift up.

Maybe it was uncalled-for, but it was an old reflex. I did the same thing when I was still living with my mother. Turning the house upside down, looking for Valium, Prozac, Xanax, Vicodin, anything that might have explained why she was the way she was. When I finally found her cache and flushed everything in hopes that she'd stop using, she only got worse. She was tearing out her hair, wringing her hands like she wanted to break them, scratching her arms until she drew blood. It wasn't long before she was throwing anything she could lay hands on in my face. She said things I don't ever want to remember. It hurt so much not to be loved, and I deserved it.

In Thomas's house, there's nobody to call me all the names under the sun. A ghost of a man can't hurt you the way a woman who's not herself anymore can. A woman who's been a child, a girl, then a mother, and who, when I left her, was just a husk, practically a corpse, with only rage and pain keeping her going. I went through Thomas's house from top to bottom, and because everyone has at least one secret, I finally found a little notebook with a red cover. It was wrapped in a bit of leather, hidden up high, on top of a rafter, and inside it were truths about Thomas's life that Benedict had no idea about.

BENEDICT

When Pa asked me to go look for Thomas, I didn't think that was fair at all. I'd never left Alaska and I didn't want to know anything about Outside, about the rest of the world. This place was more than enough for me and I couldn't see why Thomas didn't think so too.

When we were teens, he changed all of a sudden. We weren't thick as thieves like before. He didn't do the same old things anymore. He wouldn't come along with Pa and Cole when we went hunting or fishing. At fourteen he had his nose in whatever book he'd ordered through Roy, because he had read and reread all the books Ma had brought from her old schoolteacher days. He got fed up with how little schooling we'd gotten. Ma felt bad and kept saying sorry, which just got Pa riled up. I had no idea why he was making such a big deal. There was enough to learn without having to open a book.

Thomas also got it in his head to stop eating animals. He said that we didn't need to steal other lives for the sake of our own, that we could live off of plants. Like Alaska's climate was any good for a garden. Ma racked her brains to feed him, and I got a bit of a kick out of eating grilled meat in front of him, getting the juices and fat all over my hands. At first, he still wanted it but he held back, and, deep down, I did have respect for that.

He was my older brother, my only brother, I'd have been happy to follow in his footsteps until my dying breath. He wasn't like the rest of the family, while I was the spitting image of Pa—like father, like son. And yet I could see that our pa didn't look at him the same way he did me.

Thomas was already a whole, self-contained man. I wasn't even three years younger, but I was still just a teen, rough around the edges. That's what got between us, little by little, and seeing as how there weren't many folks around these parts, it caught me by surprise.

Maybe it was meant to be in the end. I suspect Thomas was made for leaving and I was made for staying. Except, when he left, he forced me to leave, too, and I had to go where I didn't want to, into civilization. The only thing

I know for sure is that he wasn't any happier there than I was.

Pa said I should try the "Mayer network." That was what he called it. I didn't have high hopes, but who else was there to try? Beginning with the branch from which we were descended, the first Mayer who had planted a flag here had been fruitful and multiplied. His children, then his grandchildren, had put down roots across America. As if he had been planning to settle the whole country, only eastward.

I couldn't believe it but, little by little, over a year, I managed to retrace my brother's tracks, going down to California, across New Mexico, Texas, Arkansas, going up and down from Illinois to Ohio, North Carolina to Virginia, and finally stopping more than three thousand miles from home in New York. For me, it was the farthest-away place in the world, but that was where I ended up, thanks to this "Mayer network," with word-of-mouth conversations, secret peeks at airline ledgers, investigations that faraway relatives I'd never met helped with, a few false starts, and plenty of true facts.

A whole clan came together for one of their own, the son of old Magnus Mayer, grandson of Augustus Mayer, great-grandson of Antoine Mayer, come straight from

France on a tiny boat my father said sunk just after reaching safe harbor, like a sign that there was no going back. They all came together, like losing one of their own might mean losing all the others. I was all alone in this country of ours, and I would never have guessed just how much a family could matter. Like some mosaic where every member's a piece and none of us can imagine the whole picture. One square was missing, and I did find one square to fill the hole, even if it wasn't the one I'd gone looking for.

FREEMAN

It was 1972 when I came back to the United States, and I could tell right away I didn't belong any more than I did when I left.

More than anything else, my family had gotten dead set on fighting for civil rights. My sisters had turned into activists: they held meetings with their "comrades in arms," as they were calling them those days, and all of them were wearing their hair natural like halos around their heads and not in the commonsense styles that they said were meant to make them look more like white women. And they weren't even one bit the homemakers they'd been when I left anymore.

Ronda and Doris got angry at me and gave me an earful for being weak, for not putting up a fight over what the white government had put me through by sending me into a war I had no business being in. I hashed things out as best as I could, saying it was my duty as an American and I'd done it. Every time I snuck out of their get-togethers with all those folks giving me side-eye, every time I said no to marching with them, Michelle said I was just the type that Whitey always dreamed of, nothing better than a good little— The word that came out of her mouth next was like a slap in the face, and she knew it.

The older I got, the more I had to allow that I'd steered well clear of that whole struggle, but back then I didn't know how I ought to act if not the way I figured a reasonable young God-fearing man should. Raising a fist, calling for action, butting heads with the police—that wasn't like me.

Once I was in the Army, I felt like I was what I ought to be: a good soldier, never mind what grand plans top brass had shipping me off to battle. I did it for America, even if America didn't do all that much for me after I came back.

So I found myself a job stocking shelves at one of those new supermarkets that had just opened and I got my own apartment. That did all of us good. It was just a small studio, not much more in it than a bed and what have you, full of all sorts of smells from the restaurant downstairs, but for me it was paradise.

Then I met Martha one Sunday at Pastor Williams's service. We saw each other for months and then we tied the knot. She was like me, well-behaved and quiet, and, as God is my witness, she was the only woman I ever had eyes for. Leslie came along a few years after our wedding and the doctors said that Martha couldn't have a second child: another pregnancy would be too much for her heart. That was just how it was—what was there to say? We accepted this decision the Lord had made because He had given us so much already. A son was more than enough, and for a long while that was the truth of it. But all things are fleeting, especially happiness.

BESS

The wind stopped all of a sudden. If I remember right, Benedict said that sometimes happens in the middle of a blizzard. Everything goes calm for a minute and that's actually more dangerous than the storm because you drop your guard, you don't keep your wits about you anymore.

I'm in front of Thomas's house. It's almost as clear now as on a sunny day. Just a few steps up, and then maybe my search will be over. I'll find the kid bundled up under a blanket and everything'll be nice and quiet in my head again. I'm scared to walk up. Better to stay in this exact moment, right before I know, while anything could still be possible, even if that's just an illusion.

I know perfectly well that nothing's the same anymore at this point—that he'll be there or he won't—and that's got my head swimming. I know that feeling all too well. It's like being on a tiny bike at the top of a hill that's steeper than anything you've ever seen. It's a drop that just keeps going down and down and down. You think that maybe you can stop but it's too late already: there's no stopping. And once you've fallen, you'll remember everything, down to the last detail, for once you'll have photographic memory. Every single thing in the background: *snap*, the mossy tree; *snap*, the calm sky; *snap*, the dog that's come out barking.

I can remember it like yesterday: the blue gate the neighbors had at the end of the lane leading to the subdivision, so that it would feel like it was ours alone, even if all that held it shut was a cheap latch. I remember the paint peeling off and the bit of wood Mr. Gillis had knocked loose when he overshot his parking spot and his old Chevy jumped the curb. I remember walking down the lane, which was more of a dirt path, going past the Douglasses' and my classmate Marisa Esposito's front yard. I remember smiling when I saw her mother's old dog dozing on the lawn and opening just one eye as I walked by. I also remember seeing that light pink Converse with a bit of the American flag across it. Lying flat, in the middle of the path, like a toy boat washed up on a beach. I remember wondering what that shoe was doing there all by itself and thinking that it looked like one of her shoes but without giving it much more thought, the sky was so blue and I felt so happy. But, at the back of my mind, the gears were already turning, trying to find an explanation for that abandoned thing. As I got closer to our yard, I realized that it wasn't really all by itself—that, a bit farther off, against the side of the porch, there was the other shoe, still on its owner's foot. A smooth child's calf, a bit more tanned than the thigh, which looked awfully pale, and then, farther up, white shorts and a Pink Floyd T-shirt, her favorite band, like she always said. I remember wondering why she was lying there, on the ground, with her eyes staring off somewhere I couldn't pinpoint.

You can push things away, but they'll always come back to you, just like that. When I finally connected the dots, I was terrified, a sort of electric shock ran through me, from the bottom of my spine to the nape of my neck, and all it left behind was a void. I ran over to her body, I picked up her head, her soft blond hair like silk in my hands, I yelled her name to bring her back from the depths of hell, but it was too late.

I'll open this door and it'll still be too late. I'm only ever able to come after, when the worst has already happened.

COLE

Why I'm still trucking through this mess I don't know. It's not my family. Don't have one, don't need one. Never wanted to be saddled with a lady, and since that's what it takes to have kids, I don't have any of those either.

Women are trouble. No pleasing 'em. Like the Lord made them imperfect just to drive us crazy. And now they want everything men have, too: the same work, the same pay, the same rights, like they can't see they're different. Anyone can tell they're not made the same. They're weak and whiny and they don't know what real brotherhood looks like. Clifford heard some tourists going on and on about how they wouldn't take being called "Miss" anymore, only "Ms." So they wouldn't be treated any different from married ladies. Now, that's a real laugh.

They're loony, no matter where they are. Married or not, all women are trouble.

When they're hitched, though, at least there's a man to remind them that God made men first. And I'm talking about real men, not those hippie folks who have to let out all their feelings or even claim women are the same as men.

I don't need to be hearing about that. I've known Benedict since he was a baby, but now I'm not too sure where he fits. His father took a chance on me by letting me work for him when I wasn't from around here and the jobs were drying up after the sawmill was shuttered. He didn't mince words, he just gave me the facts: hard work, thankless work, not much money in it, no prospects to speak of.

But I stayed all the same, even when the last machines stopped, when they were broken down so they could be shipped off to another forest, when the last guy left and the weeds started poking up across the barracks. No place for me to go and too much time on my hands meant I just had to stick with Magnus. Even his shadow taught me something.

With a father like that, Benedict grew up like a real man. At least, that was what I'd thought. With that stupid girl in a miniskirt, I don't recognize him no more. He acts a fool. Doesn't look her in the eyes, doesn't bang his fist on the table, just lets her do whatever she gets it in her head to do, dancing in the living room with her stupid music, like she's possessed. And now he's gone looking for her when what that little miss really needs is a bullet in each leg so she stops dancing like the devil.

If we find her alive, I don't know if I can keep that gun from going off. Benedict will just have to find himself another woman to look after the kid, and if she's lucky, she'll know where her place is.

BENEDICT

I got into Penn Station at the end of August 2005 with just forty dollars to my name, five dried sausages, and three rolls the Mayer-Cravens had stuffed in my backpack before I left Vermont. I said no to the beer. Not that I don't drink—Thomas wouldn't touch a drop of that stuff—but I couldn't risk anyone making off with my stuff while I was on the train. Come to think of it, that wasn't much of a good reason, seeing as I didn't have anything a thief would care about, but I'd gone clear across the USA, from a place almost nobody lived in to a massive city so full of people, I thought I'd never get a moment's peace.

Getting off the train, the heat was something I couldn't believe. I'd been through temperatures like that in California and Texas and elsewhere along the way. But that day the whole city slow-roasted me, asphalt sticking to my soles like chewing gum. A furnace that cooked me right there and sucked up every drop of saliva in my throat. I was so tired after that whole trip and I had no idea how humans could bear it, but all around me they seemed to think it was normal to live in a city like this, as hot and sealed-off as a greenhouse, with the sun bouncing off the glass skyscrapers and this heat that could turn us to toast.

I managed to find the subway and, thank God, go in the right direction. All I had was a last name and an address and I went there, telling myself that, whatever I found there, that was the end of the line for me. I'd crossed the country from west to east and I wasn't going any farther, what with this ocean I didn't know. In the subway, people wouldn't look at me, they stayed far away. With my huge beard, my hair a mess, and my raggedy backpack, they probably figured I was one of those guys who lived on the street and who had forgotten how to be civilized, and, I'll say it, that was probably what I was right then, a bit. Sitting there, I wasn't completely Benedict, son of Magnus and Maud Mayer, but some lost soul, from a faraway place who had no idea why he was there. I didn't hold that against them, I was at loose ends from having to travel so much and for so long, from having to keep going when it wasn't in my nature and I was a man of a single place: my house in Alaska.

When I got out of the subway, I walked for a while before I found the address, people ran off whenever I tried to ask for directions. I finally clapped eyes on the right building but I couldn't bring myself to ring the bell. It was my last chance to find him, to bring him back or go home alone.

I sat down across the street, right on the ground, at the foot of a tree so scraggly compared to those around my own house that I almost had to laugh. I ate two sausages and a roll. I was thirsty, but I didn't have it in me to move anymore. I dozed off for a minute and I think I really did look like what those people on the subway took me for: a man on his last legs, with too little money to get back on the straight and narrow.

I woke up, and the sun was hidden behind the buildings. The heat wasn't much less stifling, but there was a bit of a breeze that seemed to be the only real human and welcoming thing in this city. I got up, I tried to smooth down my beard, I ran my fingers through my hair and pulled it back, and I went and pressed the buzzer. After a minute a woman's voice came through. I said that my name was Benedict, that I was the brother of Thomas Mayer, and that I'd come to take him back to our parents. There was a long pause and then I heard the building door unlock as the voice told me to go up to the fifth floor. When I got to

the landing, she was waiting for me. All she had on was a
T-shirt she'd thrown on over her jeans. She was barefoot,
and her red hair was like a fire crackling around her head.
I immediately thought he had to have liked her and I felt
a bit jealous, like he'd always gotten the better end of the
deal as the older brother. She looked at me with her face
all screwed up, the way she did when she was thinking.
She stared at my face like she could find an answer to her
questions in it, and then at long last she said, "So, you're
Benedict? You've come a long way." And she had a sweet
smile on her face.

I didn't know if I'd finally found what I was looking for,
but I did want to put down my bag for a minute and catch
my breath, right there where Thomas was. Or had been.

FREEMAN

The wind isn't blowing as hard as before. I like that better.

Anyone can see I have no business being here. I should be thousands of miles away, paying off my debt. She said sending me here was a form of punishment, too, and even if saying that was in her self-interest, she wasn't all that wrong. She's had her fair share of hurt. I'm alone with my shame, with my memories I remember perfectly. Alone with pain as sharp as a sword, and most of the time there's nothing to distract me from it.

With weather like this, the boy won't be coming to see me. I figure he's really coming to see Cornelia, any kid's more excited to see a dog than an old man. Back when I was his age, I liked animals too. Having one, though—that was out of the question. One mouth too many for my mother to feed. To take my mind off of that, she took me to services every Sunday and, after school, forced me to go spend time with old folks older even than I am now, who had so much hair in their ears it gave me the shivers to imagine looking like them one day.

I spent my life trying to live up to both my mother's expectations and the Lord's teachings. Even when I passed the police entrance exam and started on my first job in Miami—even when cops who missed the old days when the only way a Black man was coming into a police station was in handcuffs tried to pick fights with me—I never lost my cool or my faith. I didn't hate them. What use would it be? They'd been raised that way. And most of them hadn't been through 'Nam, or at least not how I had. The chief, though, he'd been through the same damn war. He knew we were both part of the same special club, the club of men who couldn't sleep at night anymore and who looked over Saturday-night gunshot wounds subconsciously comparing them to the ones made by Kalashnikovs, wondering just like back then: Did they die on the spot, or did they watch their guts spill out and try to shove them back in before taking one last breath?

In this city, all I saw was a bad copy of the violence and fear that I'd been through years before, when I was just a youngster. It was like a cheap imitation of what had once been, with no life in it. I got out of that hell better than most. I didn't drown my sorrows in booze, I never looked away from a messed-up body, I didn't blink twice when I had to declare a death—didn't even wobble when some lady punched me in the gut with all the rage she had at losing her man because she couldn't put words to her hurt.

All that just got me remembering things again: the family of Samuel Uhlman, one of the few friends I had in Vietnam, when I gave them his ID tag in Queens, since I couldn't bring them back their son. The way his mama had stroked this twisted bit of metal, brought it to her lips as she sobbed over this little thing, barely any longer than a lighter and no thicker than a subway token. It was the only thing left of her son, an object that had stayed close to his skin until he died. She grabbed me in her arms the way only mothers can, and I felt like a fake because I'd survived.

Now I'm watching over something still alive and I'm keeping my promise. After this, God can send me all the torments He wants: I won't put up any fight. I'm too tired for that.

COLE

The wind fell, there's maybe three or four hours of calm before it picks up again. Unless it's the end of this damn storm. Looks like the last of winter, but I could be wrong.

I pulled out my nice binoculars, the ones I bought off of a soldier who couldn't hold his booze. Bit of a stretch to say "bought," though. More that he was snoring like a freight train and I left four beer bottles by his head as I left. Too much booze for a guy his size. Four bottles—that's hardly worth the trouble he'd get into for losing a piece of equipment, but that'll learn him. Way I see it, my taxes paid for those binoculars, so they're just as much mine as his. Never mind that I'm not really paying taxes these days. No government man's ever come around these parts to demand money I don't owe. Benedict loves saying taxes are for infrastructure, but the path down to my place is all my doing. I don't ask anything of other folks, so they shouldn't bother asking anything of me, least of all my money.

I squinted to see if I could pick out anything, but everything was white, like a huge blanket thrown over the whole world. But there have to be things hidden under it: treasures or corpses.

Then I saw Benedict sitting on a rock, staring off. A sad sight, that. No telling what had him sadder, not knowing where the kid could be or feeling so powerless. It wasn't like him not to know what to do. He'd always been sharp as a tack. When he was little, he always had to be doing whatever the grown-ups were doing, never mind how many bumps and bruises that meant. Magnus had carved two toolboxes for his sons that he'd filled with kid-size tools he'd made himself. Benedict liked anything that went fast and made lots of noise, while Thomas was more the sort to stand back a bit, take it all in, then, once he'd figured out what the guy cutting planks or polishing a piece of wood for an order was up to, he took his little tool kit and got down to help. Always so serious. Always so focused.

Handsome as an angel, too, with that curly hair that Maud wouldn't dream of cutting getting in his eyes. Now, that's a picture: some cherub falling from the sky and landing here, in the middle of the forest—but everybody here said it was sheer luck. No wives or kids around, so why not watch this boy with skin like buttercream play? It was a nice sight, and I wasn't the only one who was mighty appreciative.

BESS

He's not there.

I'm not all that surprised, but I really was hoping that a ten-year-old boy had found his way through the snow, the cold, and the wind, to end up here and wait for me while reading *Lord of the Flies*.

Silly me, thinking that something could turn out right, when luck's never on my side no matter what I do. I didn't even manage to get Benedict to love me, even though he doesn't have all that many options for miles and miles around. He looks at me like I'm not all human, like I'm beyond him. When our hands touch at the table, he jolts. Does he not think I'm real? Sometimes when he has more to drink than he ought to with Cole, I feel like he looks at me differently. There's something darker in his eyes. I've hoped it was lust, but all he's ever done is kiss my neck in July on his birthday. We had a bit to drink at lunch to celebrate. I was a bit tipsy. I was sitting by the lake, wrapped in my bath towel, because I knew Clifford couldn't be far off, watching me. Benedict was sitting next to me. We didn't say anything for a minute, and just being with him was enough while the kid was yelling since Cole had splashed cold water on him. As I was hoping that Cole would end up falling into the lake and drowning, Benedict leaned over and planted a kiss on my neck. It was a stolen kiss, like a teenager's, but a kiss that must have burned him because he jumped down to the water, pulled off his T-shirt and pants, and dived in so fast, all I saw was his back and that skin that was so pasty, considering that he was an outdoorsman.

Now that I've lost the kid, there's no chance of other kisses, other touches here and there, unless it's so he can choke me—not that I'd blame him for it.

BENEDICT

Her name was Faye Berger. She taught at Columbia University—"comp lit" was what she called the stuff she taught—and she met Thomas back in January, one afternoon when the wind and the snow were coming down so hard, she took shelter in the Metropolitan Museum of Art. The Oceania wing was empty, there was nobody but a man who'd been staring at Polynesian canoes for so long that she ended up going over and asking him if he was thinking of crossing the Atlantic with that kind of boat.

He just gave her a smile and it was his eyes that stopped her, those brown eyes with bits of gold in them and that face with its nose and wrinkles and lines almost like a woman's. He was tan like a sailor who'd been at sea for months. She said seeing him gave her a feeling she'd never been able to put her finger on, that it felt like she'd met him before and he'd been waiting for her by the slanting glass windows. He was so calm, and it was nothing like the heavy wind hitting the panes and the whistling she could hear outside. She took that stranger back to her place: her mother had taught her to always be safe but she decided to forget all that, she wasn't a girl anymore. They stayed up the whole night talking. She wanted to know what brought him down to the Lower 48 and then from one end of it to the other, and what he'd seen along the way.

He told her about the flat, dry stretches of land after snowy tundras, the grassy plains after the mountains, the deserts, and the cities with their silvery spikes, the WASPs and African Americans and Mexicans and Japanese who were all more American than he was, with names of every kind that made him think of Asia, the Middle East, Europe, food made from scratch and vegetables picked in the fields at dawn.

He also told her things I didn't know: that he couldn't stay in the same place, like some fruit that fell from a tree, since life was a constant stream: it could be a trickle or a torrent, but it was always flowing toward other things, other places, other people, other lives. He said he'd lived in the same place for so long that, nowadays, just feeling the wind when he ran or on long bus trips was enough to make him happy. He wanted to keep going and going and going, he didn't ever want to stop. Faye said it looked like he was running away and that when people go somewhere else, they're just dragging their problems along, no matter what they are, and that there are ways to solve them without having to cross a continent.

That made Thomas burst out laughing. He told her that, back home, our father would have sooner drowned a shrink in the lake with a big rock tied around his ankles than let a single member of his family get "psychologized." Thomas wasn't running away. He was hunting out new images, views he'd never seen before, so that he could give his mind something to stand in for the things he loved best, something to fill all the empty space and push out all the rest, the darkness, everything terrible about life. He wanted as much beauty as possible so there wouldn't be any ugliness left in his head.

All those things that Faye told me that night didn't feel one bit real. I almost couldn't make out my own brother in those words, but maybe we never really do know people. And the more I think on it now, I still don't know whether he was running away from something. All I know is not even that city and the people living in it could keep him in one place.

COLE

The minute he saw that the storm'd died down, Benedict wanted to go back and get the machine. I told him that was just as stupid as trying to find them on foot because we weren't even sure the wind wouldn't start blowing as hard as before and then that'd be his rig stuck in a ditch. But there was no talking sense into him.

He wasn't stupid, far from it, but it was like he took leave of his senses. Now he just about had a devil's head: the cold turned his cheeks red and his beard was thick like he'd become a bear. He was sitting in his living room, snow caked on his jacket and pants, and a hell of a puddle at his feet. Probably didn't even notice.

The kid had to be dead at this point, I'd bet good money on it. A shame, he looked like his grandfather and his uncle, even if he didn't have their common sense.

When Magnus opened his door for me, I cottoned on plenty fast that here people never ask you where you come from. You could have gotten right out of the armpit of hell or come straight from heaven, it didn't matter. If you're ready to live in the middle of nowhere, to work hard no matter the weather, and never pipe up, then you've got a place here.

That suited me: I had no shortage of things I wanted swept under the rug. Can't make an omelet without breaking a few eggs. I came from Minneapolis but I couldn't stay there long. I was done with towns where there's always someone on your back and cops watching your every step. Nobody wipes the slate clean in places like those.

Here the only fellow watching anyone else is old Clifford. He can't help himself, he even sleeps with his binoculars and his gun nearby just in case. Won't be Clifford watching me here: we've got a handshake agreement. The moonshine he brews might be undrinkable, but at least it's free and it gets people talking. We came to see that we weren't all that different from one another, even if we weren't born in the same place and it was no accident that we'd both ended up here, in a place where we could be whatever we liked, as we liked, without anyone giving us trouble.

The fact is that we were perfectly happy until Benedict came back with the girl and the kid, and that stirred up all sorts of things. We were done turning a blind eye, and now whatever happens to them happens.

FREEMAN

When Leslie was six, I got transferred to Fort Lauderdale and we moved into our very first house. We raised him the same way we'd been raised, with the love of God. He was a good little boy, always happy and always behaving himself. We only had the one, but he was even more wonderful than either of us had ever hoped. I told him about the war I'd been through like it was a movie, I told him about all the friends I'd never really had and about the hand of God, which had always been with me and protected me and which I praised every day for having allowed me to return, to marry his mother, and to have him, our treasure. Leslie listened to me, wide-eyed, and he played out the scenes he imagined me living through with his G.I. Joes. Of course, he didn't know a thing about all the blood, the remains, the guys who didn't die until they were drained dry, all the horrors no young boy should ever know about.

I did my best to pass down the values that had been passed down to me—courage, honesty, uprightness—which were the mark of an good man. When he got a bit older, he started picking up on how my being a policeman wasn't as nice as being a soldier: people had plenty of respect for veterans but not cops. I told him that one was just as good as the other, but I could see he wasn't so sure about that, and at that point I told him about the Army because that was what he wanted to hear about. I had no way of guessing that I was digging his grave.

Over the years, as I painted him a rosy picture of a war that wasn't anywhere near that rosy, as I always made sure to pay respect to the flag raised in front of the house and to America, leader of the free world, I was planting a poisonous little seed in his head that he would water all through his school years. He was the best student in his year, he was tall and skinny just like his mother, with a sweet smile, and all the girls batted their eyes at him. But rather than go to college or trade school and get married and give us grandchildren, he told us that he wanted to join up and serve his country just like I had.

I ought to have taken his decision as a sign of respect, seen it as a son showing his love for his father, but I didn't. It had been so many years that I'd forgotten it, but right there and then I tasted copper in my mouth.

BESS

I'd really like to sleep the way I did back then. After I found her body, I fell deep asleep for two days straight, with no interruptions other than a few times bolting awake, my sweat-drenched T-shirt sticking to my body and reality like a slap to my face.

Mommy never understood how I could sleep after what had happened, and I think she never forgave me for it—that, and the fact that I'd left my sister all alone.

I slept and my dreams were full of Cassandra still alive, playing a video game, her feet on the table, asking me if I was in love with Neil. Dreams where he had sex with me again, like that afternoon, in his bedroom, with those football things on the wall.

It hurt at first, but he was careful, he was gentle, and when he asked if I wanted to do it again, I said yes even though I was late and I had to go take my sister to dance class. I figured that it was too late anyway, that she'd miss class and all I'd get would be a slap on the wrist. She wouldn't have snitched to our parents—that wasn't her style—and she knew that it was a special day: I'd told her that I was going to become a woman. A woman? Ha! I got that idea in my head from reading all those stupid magazines Mommy brought back from the clinic she worked at. Cassandra braided my hair ever so nicely so it wouldn't fall all over the place. She asked me to tell her everything after, but I wasn't sure I would. What was I going to tell her? A stranger's hands on my skin, breathing, a boy trembling over you and crushing you? Or how silly he looked after he came, that dripping between my legs because he didn't have the condom on right? It's sheer luck I didn't get pregnant. I really wanted to lose my virginity, men made such a big deal of it but I just thought of it as a burden. A virgin, pure and innocent—that's such a silly idea.

Maybe if I hadn't cared so much about losing it, I wouldn't have lost her too. We'd be eating a slice of cheesecake, sitting on our parents' couch, talking about our children or our boyfriends. Time wouldn't have taken its toll on our lives.

But instead, when I got home, two hours late, cutting through lawns and backyards, she was already dead. Lying on the grass, her dance bag right beside her, like it was a sign. She wanted to feel grown-up, too, she wanted to go to her dance class all on her own at thirteen although she still looked eleven and Mommy said no. She met a man that day, too, but he didn't tell her about love. He just grabbed her throat, choked her, and killed her.

I'd been thinking it was the most important day of my life, and it was the last day of hers, just because a man wanted to kill. Did I sleep for two days straight after that? Yes, so the pain would stay put inside me, so it would seep into every cell of every organ and become one with me, a girl who'd broken her promise for some short-lived pleasure I didn't even get.

BENEDICT

I lived with Faye for weeks after I showed up. I hunkered down in her apartment all day because of that loud, stinky city that never stopped fidgeting. I only poked my nose out in the evenings, and even after dark the streets were still too busy for my taste.

That made her smile. She said my brother had been a wild bear, but I was even wilder. He at least had been okay going outside with her, meeting people, visiting museums, or even just walking down the street, looking around at everything.

I didn't care what Thomas managed to do or not do: he and I weren't the same, I knew that already. I'd never have up and left without so much as a look back.

It took me days on end to decide whether I ought to write my parents and tell them that I was coming back but alone, or not say a thing and give them at least a bit more time to hope that I'd found him. I took the easy way like a coward: I didn't do anything—and I ended up wishing I hadn't.

Because I wouldn't go outside most of the time, Faye brought over friends or colleagues once or twice a week, maybe so she'd civilize me. They were New York women, but they were all shapes and sizes—tall, thin, short, squat— so that I got to wondering if all the civilizations of the world had been thrown in a bowl and tossed together and that was what made all these funny combinations. Some looked at me funny and one of them even said I was exotic. I didn't really see what she meant. I was just a man from the Far North, while she was a tall, wiry woman with long, shiny blond hair that smelled like lilacs. Her skin was so thin that it probably wouldn't have taken anything to make her veins burst. While Faye was in the kitchen, she whispered that I should come over for dinner sometime and I had no idea what to say. She was easy on the eyes, sure, but I just stared at the thin white hand she put on my arm and I didn't say a thing. That can't have been very good manners on my part. She made a face and pulled her hand back as soft as she'd stuck it out.

I hadn't met many women, just enough to know that they were so much more complicated than men. I had trouble understanding what they wanted, what was hiding under their words. I thought their words always meant two things at the same time until I met Faye, whose words were as honest as her feelings.

It didn't take me long to understand why Thomas had stayed with her, why he'd fallen in love with a woman who didn't have to do anything more than smile. But that hadn't been enough to keep him there. It was just sheer chance that he'd left at the end of July, almost a month to the day before I turned up. She came home one afternoon and found a note saying he was leaving, he couldn't stay longer. She knew he didn't like planes and he only had the money from his odd jobs, so she figured he must have taken a boat because he wanted to leave the United States. He could just as easily be on a cargo ship as on one of those Caribbean islands, but I was sick and tired of looking for him. I couldn't stop living my own life just to run after a ghost that didn't want to be found.

BESS

I've come here so many times I know Thomas's house just as well as my own. Benedict only agreed to talk about it once. He said his brother was just eighteen when he said he wanted to live on his own, in a house all his own, so he could live by his own rules. He wanted to settle in the original Mayer house, a run-down shack set back a bit from the lake. It was a one-room log cabin like in those picture books about the American frontier—a real childhood dream, I suppose. The roof was caved in, probably from so much snow, but the walls were still standing.

His father wasn't happy, because it was a dangerous spot, too close to the crevasses cutting through the rocks east of the lake. It wasn't for nothing that his forebears had chosen to build their second house in a safer location. But Magnus did respect his son's decision and helped him to build an add-on so he could have an actual bedroom.

His parents were sure he wanted to start a family. I realized it wasn't to have kids that he'd moved there, but I never said as much to Benedict.

Daddy taught me many years ago never to be the bearer of bad news, you could get your head cut off that way. Sometimes you don't even need to say a word. I can still see the look on Mommy's face when she came home, with the police cars in the street, the officers coming and going and the one talking to me very nicely with a hand on my shoulder. Her eyes as she saw my head, as she saw Daddy sitting on the couch, sobbing, and her eyes when she looked through the French door and saw they'd set a body on the stretcher, such a small body in a big bag with a zipper that had been yanked shut so fast we could almost hear it inside. Zipped all the way up because she didn't need to breathe anymore. Right then, I thought Mommy wouldn't ever breathe again, that all the blood was gone from her body. The one thing every parent's most scared of had happened to her. She let out a long, wild scream and that scream is still the most terrifying thing I've ever heard.

I stayed for the autopsy results, for the police visits, for all the friends, neighbors, acquaintances, for the funeral, but also for the long stretches without anyone, when the grief was so heavy that my parents couldn't even be together in the same room anymore. I stayed when Daddy couldn't bear her look anymore, when the two of us were alone, and when she was saying every day that it was my fault, that I should have been watching my sister, that I'd broken my promise. I stayed when she started taking more Valium, Xanax, alcohol to wash them down, and then, when that wasn't enough anymore, morphine she'd stolen from the clinic, until they realized how much medicine was missing and fired her, saying that they could understand her pain and they sympathized, they really did, but that they couldn't look the other way.

Look the other way. Not see. Wouldn't that be nice? I'd love to do that. But I stayed for everything, the fall from grace, the downfall, down to the moment I had to say goodbye to the woman I knew, as I'd known her, because I didn't recognize what was there anymore. In her more lucid moments, she said that she wanted me to go, just seeing me was too much. I wasn't a good girl, someone had gotten things mixed up, made a mistake by leaving me alive and not Cassandra.

I left, because that was what she wanted. I was eighteen. I dropped out, I didn't have a dollar to my name. I sold what I still had of my girlhood—my jewelry, even the golden necklace I'd gotten for my fifteenth birthday—and I bought a bus ticket to the middle of nowhere. I had my mind made up to erase every trace of Elizabeth Morgensen, the girl who didn't save her sister, and I became Bess, just Bess. And maybe even that's still too much.

FREEMAN

Leslie enlisted that same year. He was in the Marines for four years and he was barely any older than I'd been in Vietnam when he deployed to Iraq for another far-off war. He stayed with his unit, and Martha and I followed his tracks on a world map with a small red dot just about where his base was. Words on a map that didn't mean a thing to us, just some bit of exotic color that was nothing to do with reality, although that did stave off our worries a bit. He was far away and it could just as easily have been the land of Scheherazade and not some desert.

Martha worried herself sick, but she was still proud of her son. She would sit on the porch, her Bible in her lap, and the neighbors, Black and white alike, would greet her and talk with her as if we had sent the Messiah to the Holy Land. I feared that he might have been sent to hell like myself, but I bit my tongue. The times were different, and so were the places, the soldiers didn't have half as much blood to deal with.

But even with all these newfangled technologies, men would always find ways to wound, to slash, to hack at their brethren, that was just in man's nature. War would stay war. Sowing terror, rallying people. It made killing other human beings seem okay just because you'd been told that there was good reason to, just because you were the good guys fighting the baddies. There's always some good reason behind our children getting blown up by land mines or coming back in slings, quiet as the grave and not putting one word to what they've seen.

Leslie came home after only a few months, his knee in pieces after an IED went off under his convoy. His higher-ups said he'd been lucky. Others hadn't survived. The military still shipped him back to us: damaged goods. He couldn't fight anymore, he could barely walk, his career was over before it'd really started.

Martha was as sad as she was relieved. He was back in one piece, she kept saying, not dead in a sealed coffin. And I was of the same mind: that we were lucky to have our son back. A father and a mother won't always understand that a boy who's been made a man far too fast is more than a knee, some crutches, and plenty of stumbling: there's his mind and all the top secret things that were put in it. Go pills so he won't sleep, to feel invincible while fighting, all sorts of meds he'd been told to take without knowing what they were because soldiers follow orders. Was there a doctor saying it was for their well-being? That it was just a little pick-me-up like what retirees knock back to feel good? Back then I wasn't too sure what exactly he'd taken, but after the nightmares I chalked up to his fighting, after his weeks of insomnia, his bouts of delirium, after he'd taken the neighbors' dog and snapped its neck with his crutch because it wouldn't stop its barking, I had to allow that the man who'd come back from Iraq wasn't the one who'd shipped off. A stranger in my house, nothing like that naked baby set on his mother's belly and taking his very first breath who'd made our lives a good sight better than ever before. War snatched up our son and gave us back a photograph negative: some white shadow on a background blacker than black.

BENEDICT

At the end of September, I told Faye I had to leave. It was best that I get back home before it was deep winter.

She seemed off. I could tell something wasn't right, but I'd never been much of a psychologist, least of all when it came to women.

The morning I left, as I was pulling together the few belongings of mine, she showed me why Thomas had left. She didn't need to say a word, she just took my hand and set it on her belly. When I figured it out, it was like an electric shock. She said Thomas sounded happy at first, well and truly happy. They'd spent nights talking about the future, thinking about names and where they'd live. He went to get steady work, to provide for the baby, it was time for him to start a family and for him to stop traveling the world. But just as fast as he'd gotten pulled in, he'd gone quiet. He ended up leaving, overnight, without any explanation apart from the note he'd scribbled in the entryway. He didn't want to be a father.

I felt so ashamed when Faye showed me that sad scrap of paper. He'd written those words on the back of a takeout menu, like it was just a shopping list, just some business to take care of. And she kept that bit of paper anyway, like a souvenir of Thomas—not the nicest one, not the best one, just something with his handwriting on it.

Living in this mess of a city weighed on me, but I told her that I'd stay until the baby was born, that I'd say I was the father, and that he'd keep the Mayer name because that made him part of a clan that would never forget him or abandon him. Faye kicked up a fuss—it wasn't what she'd wanted—but I told her that my mind was made up and that I wasn't going to be talked out of it. I went with her for the ultrasounds and the doctor visits, I left the shelter of her apartment to do odd jobs, to help her out with bills, to get furniture for the baby's room, to get decent health insurance. And then I held her hand through the contractions, I wiped the sweat off her forehead, I watched her fight a battle fiercer than I'd ever have guessed, and when the baby was born, I cut the umbilical cord as if he were my own son. Which he needed to be.

I swore to myself I'd love him the way I loved the free and brave woman that his mother had been, the way I loved her even though we'd never been lovers. I had no chance with someone like her, after all. My brother had taken up all the empty space in her heart, he'd filled in every nook and cranny, as she was so fond of saying. There was no room left for me, but that didn't matter in the end. I was used to him getting all the attention as if he were the only source of light anywhere. Living in his shadow, orbiting around him, half in the light and half in the dark, didn't bother me all that much, as long as my father loved me. Not more than my brother, but at least as much as him.

When the baby was born, the only thing Faye and I didn't agree on was his name. She wanted to call him Thomas, and I wasn't going to give him the name of a man who'd run away, not even if he was my own brother. But I let that woman have her way, seeing as all this was because of her love.

COLE

I let Benedict go get his machine and I went home. Starting that rig was no easy matter in the best of times, so I didn't figure he'd get anything done in this weather.

I'd started pulling off all my gear when I heard crackling over the CB radio that made me change my mind.

Clifford said he'd seen the woman go into Thomas's house across the lake. She was safe and warm in there without the boy, and he was itching to go and drop in on her if Benedict wasn't headed over, just to show her one or two things a man could do with a girl.

I told him not to wait for me, he could go and do as he liked, and in any case Benedict was too busy fiddling with his machine to bother the two of them.

Come to think of it, I wouldn't mind giving that bitch something to remember too.

I told Clifford that I'd meet him and that he should do whatever he wanted before I got there. He hadn't had his way with a woman in ages. That's a rare sight around these parts, a woman who wants sex—although Clifford's not in the habit of asking them in the first place. A man's got his needs, pure and simple.

I figured that, with him, Bess would get a good fifteen minutes she'd never forget. She'd been asking for it, what with her skirts and those shorts that didn't do anything to cover her up. And all Benedict cared about was finding his son, not some girl who'd lost him. Time to teach him a little something.

I grabbed my rifle and went out the back door in case Benedict saw. I cut through the brush behind the house. The visibility was nothing like the past few hours: it was still snowing—gusting hard, too—but none of that damn wind that could lay a body out flat.

If the kid was dead—I figured as much by now— someone'd be paying for it. That's what old Magnus always taught his sons. The bill always comes due, and when it does, one way or another, you pay up.

BENEDICT

I'd almost go so far as to say that Ma was lucky. While I was gone, she died in her sleep, the same way she'd lived, not making any trouble for anyone. Pa woke up next to her that morning and at first he didn't realize. He told Cole she looked like a little girl asleep, more calm and peaceful than she'd been in months. The doctor said that her heart had given out, just like that, nothing more to it.

But I don't think she had a weak heart. I think she was too ashamed at seeing one son leave, then the other, and that she didn't have any will to go on living. Before you have kids, you think your life is full to bursting, that its little ups and downs are enough to make you happy. And then you get some idea of how empty it'll be with them gone, when there's nothing left really worth experiencing, nothing left as wonderful as having seen them grow up, change from tottering kids to teens who'll whine about every decision you make. For me, becoming a father by accident, I didn't really think on any of it. I'd never really imagined that someday I'd have a kid, my own kid.

More than any other, little Thomas is a being all on his own, a human who's nothing like me at all. Not because I'm not his actual father, but because he's in that space between two worlds. Who is he the son of? A mother who decided to raise him on her own? A man who was such a coward that he ran off just as fast as he fathered him? I've never asked anyone those questions.

Not long after Ma died, Pa had a stroke. It happened while he was standing in the middle of the river, fishing for trout. He would have drowned if Cole hadn't managed to drag him to the bank. In the weeks after, he fed my father, washed him, talked to him every day, and sometimes wiped away his tears. By the time I came back home, Magnus was almost nothing like his old self. I tried to tell him about Thomas and the kid when we were alone. I couldn't wait to tell him that he had a grandson, that the Alaska Mayers would keep on going with a new generation here, but he barely reacted, with half his face drooping thanks to the stroke, his skin looking like a landslide. I don't know what I was expecting. He wasn't going to jump and shout for joy, I'll say that much. I don't think the news made it to his brain, and all I felt was ashamed.

I wished I hadn't kept that happiness secret from him. I could have just called, or sent a letter, so that he could have stopped fretting over his lost son and started dreaming about the baby, Thomas's son. Ma might have still been alive, at least until I came back without the child and with no explanation of why he was so far away from them, thousands of miles away, in a city that they only knew by name. I didn't tell Cole about any of that either.

Years later, when I brought the boy to his grandparents' tomb, he asked me what sort of father Magnus had been. A father who'd never failed, I said, and that only made me feel even more like an orphan.

FREEMAN

For more than a year, Martha and I tried everything. We saw doctors, shrinks, veteran groups. I read everything I could lay hands on to put words to what had happened to our son, to make heads or tails of why he'd come back wrecked like that.

His bitterness I could understand: war spits you out in a million pieces. Nobody warns you about the dead men, about them coming and haunting you until you take your last breath. Their faces are a blur now, but you never forget the unnatural way their arms and legs went, the gashes so deep you can see the bone like someone wanted to show you how bodies worked, just because they wondered, since they wanted to see. There's also the ones whose faces are always there, and you're stunned that they're intact, despite the blows, despite the shock of death. You never forget the kids curled up on themselves or the women sleeping like time had only stopped and you could just snap your fingers to make their cheeks rosy again. I still remember every one of those faces and I reckon Leslie was no different: he could summon up every body left on the sides of the gravel roads he went up and down where all the sand was good for was soaking up their blood. That I could understand.

Hate, on the other hand—that was beyond me. Leslie would spend the night pacing around in his room and start off every morning cursing his country. He'd come down the stairs clutching the railing, not looking at his mother, who was always waiting for him in the same spot and watching for some sign that never came. That hair he'd let grow out was in box braids, like he was set on getting as far as possible from the no-name buzz-cut soldier he'd been. On his better days he filled his hours watching TV and drinking beer, on his worse days he stared at a spot over the fireplace, the photo of him in a uniform. There was nothing the man in the room and the man in the frame had in common. One Sunday, when Leslie couldn't stand to look at that photo no more, he threw that frame clear across the room. Martha rushed to clean up the shards, but Leslie yelled at her not to touch it, that if she did he'd end her.

There isn't a mother alive who could believe that her son might raise a hand against her.

Martha leaned down to at least get the photo and he stomped right on her belly. I helped my wife get up and I told my son to clear out.

He'd crossed a line and I still had no idea what exactly had gotten him in such a state. This was something far beyond those drugs that soldiers took in Vietnam to scrape along while top brass slept. No, it was worse than that: some deal America had with the devil.

It was only later on, when people started coming out with the facts, that I started seeing just how many young men and women were left a wreck by something that wasn't fighting, that it couldn't be kept bottled up. But by then it was too late for my Leslie, too late for our son.

BESS

I'm in this empty house, I'm standing still in this part of the world the way I've almost never stood still since I left Mommy's.

I promised myself never to stay in the same place for long, definitely not long enough to make friends or meet someone I could fall in love with. Just blaze through like a comet and then disappear, always leaving, always on the road. Apparently I've done every small job that's to be had in this country—respectable jobs, dirty jobs, all of them. There's no work I won't do: if it puts food on the table, it's good enough for me.

What could be more humiliating than what I've already been through? More painful or horrible than the memories and the shame I have to bear? I'm the only one who saw him and I didn't say a thing. I held the gate open for him, I had no clue he'd just killed my sister. He smiled at me and I actually batted my eyes because I thought he looked sexy under that hat covering his eyes, with his square jaw, his shiny teeth, his beach tan, his muscles. I could have done a police sketch, told you what he was wearing, his height and weight. But I didn't, because I felt ashamed I'd tried to seduce her murderer. Over the years, each time I found out that a teen girl had disappeared in LA or thereabouts, I felt like I wasn't even a human, like I was made of that concrete that had covered my legs.

And as if I wasn't already hurting enough, I went looking for trouble. I baited men in bars where I was a waitress, men who could have knocked me flat with a sucker punch. I wasn't actually scared. What I really wanted was to get my face messed up, as if two wrongs would make a right. Most of the time, that stopped them: they weren't expecting me to want it. Most women aren't like that and that'll make an alpha male think twice. Sometimes I still did catch a punch, but never one strong enough to leave its mark. I got told off for poking the bear, I lost my job, and I was off again, a hothead in a woman's body.

I hopscotched all over the coast and across the Central Valley, wherever my bad rep took me. A bad girl, however you want to take it: a bad girl, a bad sister, a bad woman. I ended up in Vegas, first waiting tables in the tiniest uniform I'd ever worn in my life, then hostessing, being a tour guide, and working on the floor when I started to feel like I could breathe again. I liked working in the middle of so much: all around me were guys who were as messed up as me and didn't know it. We were all drawn to the blinking lights, the strobes catching my eye, hypnotizing me like a spiral that just kept spinning, white on black, black on white. I loved those stretches of not thinking before the shift ended and I had to face the pale daylight, the runny white light of the desert. And then everything was real again. I went home to pass out in the mobile home I shared with another girl. All I wanted was black, heavy sleep.

I was on my cigarette break one night when I saw them. I remember that hairy man-bear with a beard that swallowed up his face. Security was watching him even if they weren't totally sure why. His paw was holding a pale, smooth hand, small like a scale model, belonging to a little boy who had no idea which way to look in this twinkling city that was like a year-round Christmas display, Disneyland for grown-ups.

I still have no idea how they ended up there, but they looked so lost that I went over to them. The man stared at me like I was the first human being he'd ever met. He didn't know which hotel to stay at, they all seemed so loud and bright that he didn't dare to go through the front entrance. It wasn't about money, he was saying, it was about place. He felt out of place and he wasn't sure this was the right place for a boy. That made me smile.

I set them up in a restaurant where I knew one of the waitresses and I told them to stay put until my shift was over two hours later. I still don't know what I saw in them then. Something that stood out in this crowd, something that made me think I was seeing wrong. And it made me think that maybe history would stop repeating itself—maybe there was a loophole.

Of course, I was wrong again.

BENEDICT

I'm trying my best to get this machine working, but it's not doing a thing. I'm sweating like a pig even in this cold. How did we end up here? How was I stupid enough to bring them here?

It's killing me just how much I wasn't thinking. What did I expect, dragging the two of them to someplace so far away from anything that you can't even find it on a map? That she'd be sweet and hardworking like my mother when she never met a rule she didn't want to break? That he'd magically turn into a good Alaska boy just like me?

Faye never came here. She couldn't even dream of where we'd been raised, the way I'd grown up. She just let me leave with the boy, she didn't even ask where I was taking him. She said that even hell would be a nicer place for the boy than New York.

What was I supposed to say to a woman who knew her days were numbered? That I'd grown up a woodsman, tracking and hunting with no bigger ambitions than being like my father and Cole, not having to answer to anybody, while my brother wanted books, knowledge, and all that? At some point Thomas told me that this world was closed off and it was a prison of my own and that I didn't even care about where its walls were: I was chicken when it came to civilization. That's the one and only time we got in a brawl, a real one. I was younger but I had more strength than Thomas: I bashed in his face and Dad had to pull us apart. I hated my brother for acting like he was better than me: he could appreciate the first ray of sunlight in spring, how pretty the waves on the lake were, while all I cared about was showing my father just how much of a man I was.

I was manly enough that the thought of living alone with this boy in the city where he was born—his city, his mother's city—scared me to death. When she wrote to me years later to say that she had cancer and now her only option left was "palliative care" and that she wouldn't even make it to the end of the year, she asked me to come as quick as I could. I never thought she'd trust me with this boy who wasn't even mine, who I hadn't seen grow up. According to the law, he was my son because she and I had signed an acknowledgment of paternity, but according to other men I was just a deadbeat dad who'd hightailed it back to Alaska. We got married in the hospital room: that was what she wanted. She was pale like she was already dead. I was fidgeting in a suit I'd bought in a rush, it was so tight on me that she tried not to laugh when she saw me. It sounded like a death rattle. And the boy beside us, the little one who didn't understand anything, sitting through everything—a death he couldn't even imagine and a father who'd turned up out of nowhere.

She'd planned it all out with her lawyer. After she died, I was responsible for a boy who was too shocked to put up any fight. I also got a pretty penny from her inheritance. There'd been a lot of ugly back-and-forths over the months. Faye's mother brought in lawyers so she could get the kid, saying she was his only relative, that his actual father had never taken care of him. I didn't know a thing about that woman, just what Faye had told me, and I had no idea just how much a mother and her daughter could hate each other. The courts ruled that the kid was staying with me: Faye had made her wishes clear enough that there was no ignoring them.

I left New York, I sent back suitcases of books, schoolbooks, and two years' worth of clothes, and I drove the boy, with the things his mother cared the most about packed in two cardboard boxes. Two strangers in a rental car with nothing to say, barely even looking at each other. He thought I was his father, and the whole time I was driving I kept thinking over that lie. She'd made me swear never to tell anybody the truth no matter what, not until the kid was grown up. Since I had no idea what to do with a child, I decided we should go backward to every stop on the trip that had brought me to his mother. We went to see each of the Mayers who'd helped me years before. I wanted to show him that it was possible to fill a hole, no matter how big, with human warmth, little by little, like a measuring cup, tablespoon by tablespoon.

It wasn't much, but there wasn't much else I could do or much better I could offer him. My parents had been dead a long time and there was nobody waiting for us now.

BESS

I fell asleep in Thomas's armchair. This despair I knew so
well had gotten the better of me.

Would the boy's face fade away someday like Cassandra's? Hazy outlines, just a silhouette, and your mind
playing tricks on you: *Look, you don't remember her anymore, you can't even honor her memory now.* The boy's
still there in my head: thin shoulders, bony legs, narrow
joints making him look nothing like a lumberjack's grandson ready to be like his father and grandfather and great-
grandfather, strong, unshakable men all of them. The boy's
a total mystery. Where'd that body come from? Where'd
he get all those brains that won't do him any good in a
place like this? He's some exotic pet bird left in the wild:
no defenses, no survival skills. He tells me secrets, whispers
all sorts of things in my ear without his father knowing,

when we're both hidden under his big bed with the sheets hanging down to the ground like tent flaps. Secrets about what he thinks about this hero living in the same house as us, that bearded giant who came straight out of a myth, who could split a log as thick as a beam with a single axe blow, who could carry half an elk carcass on his shoulder or kill a bear with only one gunshot to protect his own. That descendant of Titans, who's so quiet because a witch on a rocky island in the Mediterranean cast a spell so he couldn't open his heart or he'd turn everyone he loved to stone. I liked the way the boy reinvented the story, making something out of a father-son meeting that hadn't gone perfectly, and the way he kept believing that someday Benedict would tell him how he'd met the boy's mother, tell him about their love and especially why he'd left him and his mother to live by themselves. Like there was an explanation for everything.

I woke up with a start. A dry, calloused hand was flat on my mouth. Clifford's red face was just a few inches from mine.

"Hello, Bess. You're not getting bored all by your lonesome, are you?"

His whole body was pressed up against mine, his left hand was holding down my wrists while his right hand had come down to unzip his pants.

"I'll give you what Benedict couldn't be bothered to, sweets."

I tried to bite him, to knee him, to push that heavy, unnatural body off, but he didn't let up: he kept going, nibbled, dug his fingers into my clothes, through the zippers, trying to get at my skin. I fought as hard as I could even with his forearm pressed against my belly to keep me on the chair, but I was no match. And then he had to let go of my wrists for a second to pull down my pants.

What happened in that second? What part of my brain was taking orders? What part of my body finally decided he wasn't going to have his way? I groped around, feeling with my fingertips for what I'd seen by the hearth while Clifford was already grinning at what he was sure he was about to get, smirking like the vilest sort of man.

I finally felt the steel under my palm, cold and oddly soothing, then made contact with the wooden handle, and when I had a good hold on it, I struck.

At the first blow to his temple, he stared at me, befuddled, as if he were a child surprised to have his toy taken away. Blood was dripping into his ear, darker and thicker than I'd have expected. With the second blow, it went deep into his throat, almost like a knife through butter. I pushed it in down to the handle, my hand flat on its butt end, with all the fury I had, until I felt his body go limp and slump back.

Clifford was staring straight at me. He wasn't blinking, there weren't any questions in his eyes, there wasn't a single clue as to what he'd seen when he got to the light at the end of the tunnel, if that had made his death any more peaceful.

FREEMAN

We didn't hear from Leslie for years. We had no clue where he'd gone and no way of finding out. Like he'd gone poof.

I made some inquiries, only to learn he wasn't collecting his disability pay. The VA had no leads. I figured he might be dead, just lying somewhere, like the corpses we'd left behind in 'Nam. I couldn't even broach the subject with Martha. She went to church every day, she sang and prayed like her prayers could bring back her boy.

I think it might have been at that moment that I forgot how to believe in Him. My faith in God had stood me in good stead for so long: when I was young, then when I was in the war, and even when I was trying to keep our streets nice and safe. I just stopped thinking about Him one day. God had gone quiet.

I kept going to Sunday services so as not to upset Martha even more, but my thoughts took me far off, past those walls, those songs, those bodies rocking back and forth. So as not to forget my own son, I got to volunteering every hour I could with the VA, for those banged-up men from the Gulf War and all the ongoing conflicts. There were new technologies that were supposed to be zero loss, or just about. The Department of Defense boasted about how nowadays they'd only lose a few soldiers, how nice that looked by comparison to both world wars! As if saying that helped any. Every single soldier had a family, there's no filling the hole in their lives. But not a soul was giving that any thought, not even the president himself in his Oval Office.

It was while I was going to help some poor fellow from Virginia who'd lost both legs in Afghanistan but had to prove it that I came across an old colleague, Saunders. I hadn't looked for my son in ages, but there he was again. Saunders said he'd been out at Hunts Point investigating a prostitution ring, and he'd seen Leslie there. But Leslie'd up and changed his name, or more likely his line of work called for a new one. He was going by Magic because he was selling dreams, smoke and mirrors, drugs in every shape and form. He'd been settling some scores and that was what got him put away. Walking through the police station, Saunders had seen that pretty face and recognized it straightaway from the photo in my office. It was like he hadn't aged a day. And then he was out on bail the very same day, thanks to a lawyer from the nicer part of town. Apparently he had plenty of connections: he'd really made a name for himself.

I didn't tell Martha a thing. The shame would have been the end of her. I let a whole year go by before I decided to pay a visit to New York. I lied to the woman I'd married: I told her I was going to a 'Nam vet reunion in New Jersey. It was long enough of a drive to think through every horror we'd been put through.

I couldn't help but feel that it was no thanks to my luck that he'd come back just like a boomerang, only as broken on the inside as on the outside. I stayed under a fake name in one of those run-down hotels where the staff didn't look too closely at the ID you gave them, and day after day I went up and down the streets around the police station, going a bit farther out each time. I pestered everyone I saw, asked more questions than I ought to have in this neighborhood, more questions than any old man ever ought to ask. I almost got killed a few times and maybe deep down that's what I was hoping for, for my luck to finally run out. They could have offed me and folks both here and back home would have been none the wiser. I left the hotel phone number at every bodega and every bar I passed. *Tell him to call me, it's important.* As if anything were really that important. I had an awfully good idea of what I might end up finding out, but I did it anyway, for Martha, who'd rocked her only son in her bosom and who couldn't understand.

It took six days until I finally got a call. It wasn't him but the voice of a boy pretending to be older than he was. He said Magic wanted to meet in Central Park the next night, at seven, and if I knew what was best for me I'd better knock it off with my questions. I knew it wasn't wise, but I went. I reckoned maybe I could still bring my son back home. It might be that God's hand was still with me after all, but all the same I took my gun with me, seeing as I had no way of knowing if the devil had taken His place.

Ages after the time he'd told me, just when I was getting ready to leave, Leslie turned up, and that shattered knee of his made his gait look almost casual. Somehow he'd made a dreamy thing of it. He was still a looker, but he must have developed a sweet tooth as he climbed up the ranks. His skin was grayish and his teeth were nothing like the smile he'd had as a teenager. Tattoos ran all the way up his neck to his jaw and there was no two ways about their meaning.

He kept his distance, his eyelids were heavy and low, he thrust up his chin like he was proud, and he asked what it was I wanted. What I wanted? I wanted to find my son, not some hotshot dealer. I called him by his Christian name and I told him that his mother was hoping he'd come home, that she hadn't raised her one and only son to go around poisoning people.

He spat on the ground and said he had all the dough, blow, and hoes he wanted, that his brothers looked up to him, that Leslie was dead and buried, and that, unless I was going to buy a thing or two to take care of my arthritis, I could go and fuck off and the same went for my old lady.

I don't know why I pulled out my gun. I don't know why I took aim, why I shot at my son right there and then. I think it was my failings that I was thinking on, my own failings that I wanted to snuff out. I did it because I reckoned someone had to and it had to be me because no God-fearing soul should ask anyone else to bear a cross like that on their account.

I did my son in, I wasn't able to protect him and keep him on the straight and narrow, and—owing to me, my own errors—he'd ended up poisoning other sons himself. I killed him and I don't know what else I'd have done if she hadn't turned up.

COLE

Thomas's house wasn't far off now. I took my time getting there. Hard going, sure, but also I wanted to give Clifford plenty of time to do whatever he was going to do. I didn't want to see him fucking her, that's not my sort of thing. After, when it was all over, once he'd shown her where she belonged, that would be the best part. Her humiliated, put in her place, that little slut who doesn't even deserve to be spat on. I always say you have to remind women who's in charge.

So I took my sweet time, and when I got to the house, there wasn't a peep to be heard. He was done, then. The thought went through my head that this was going to be a real headache. We'd have to come up with some explanation for Benedict as to her state, or we'd have to spell things out for her so she didn't go telling him the facts.

I went in, the door was ajar. Clifford was on the ground, hadn't even pulled up his pants, and that bastard was already asleep. No sign of that girl, she had to be blubbering somewhere. I called out to Clifford, "Well, well, well, everything fair and square now?" And he didn't say a thing, wasn't making a sound. The man snores like a chain saw every night, so maybe he was having the best snooze of his life.

I walked over and the soles of my boots stuck on the floor. I'd lived long enough to know exactly what I'd stepped in. I grabbed his shoulder to turn him over and I saw he was good and dead. His mouth was gaping and his eyes were wide-open. Thomas's wood chisel was deep in his neck.

That really set me off. Only one man around these parts really got me and he'd just been offed.

I looked up and I saw the girl in the corner and Clifford's blood all over her hands. She was like a deer in headlights.

I spat out, "You killed Clifford! You happy now?"

She didn't say a thing.

I walked over and my face was up in hers so she had to look at me and I shouted, "You couldn't just lose the kid, huh? Are you out to bump off each of us?"

She just said, "I know the truth, Cole."

"What truth?"

But I didn't have to think for long. So that was why she'd always given me the cold shoulder. And that really pissed me off. She was looking at me all superior like, the way they all did—my lawyer, the judges, the guards, even the guys in prison uniform who were no better than me but who still beat me up to teach me a lesson. Like I was a monster, but I was no worse than any of them. Fact is, nobody's ever tried to understand me, Clifford excepted. And what right did that girl have to judge me? She couldn't even be bothered to do right by Benedict and his kid.

I had no idea what to do, but I knew I couldn't let her mess up my whole life. I hadn't found this slice of heaven, made a home for myself over the years, just for some lady like her to wreck it. Absolutely not. And calling the police for them to lock her up for murdering Clifford was out of the question, so I figured the next best thing was to take care of her exactly the way he would have if she hadn't beaten him to it. I had to think fast before Benedict got it in his head to come here.

I took a step back, aimed my rifle at her, and told her to get up and scram. One of us had to disappear, and it sure wasn't going to be me. Maybe she'd want to off herself anyway after killing a man or losing the kid. I'd just be helping her along.

Benedict wouldn't argue with that, and then the two of us could go on living our own lives, almost just like before.

She stood up, didn't put up any fight, maybe she thought I was going to take her to her house. I pointed at the door with the rifle barrel. She pulled on her shoe with a scowl and walked past me just wearing her pitiful sweater and those pants she hadn't zipped up. She looked even smaller than before, and she was limping.

I wondered if Clifford at least got it in before getting killed, but I wasn't about to ask. I didn't care enough. I was the one running the show now, I was the one who said what happened next, and I'd decided to shut her up for good.

She made her way to the doorstep and I kept my rifle on her because, if she'd managed to off Clifford, I had to watch my back. I shoved her with the barrel so she'd keep moving. She went down the steps, she shivered, and for half a second I couldn't believe some little girl like her had managed to kill a man.

BENEDICT

Sometimes it's only when you stop thinking that you see what's staring you in the face. I was cursing that damn snowmachine and Thomas, who'd made us get it before he up and left, and then the lightbulb went on.

If Bess or the kid had to take shelter somewhere, the only place they'd have gone would be Thomas's house. And as if figuring that out fixed everything, the machine started rumbling. It's stupid, but it got my hopes up. Old Freeman turned up right then and I don't think I was ever so happy to see him. He said that Cornelia couldn't stand being cooped up anymore and that he'd decided to come make sure we were all right. I think he said something about it being one winter too many for him, that he wasn't going to be staying, but I was only half listening. Sure, I appreciated seeing him, but I didn't give him the details,

I didn't have the time. I just told him to make himself at home in my house, that I might need his help when I got back. Cornelia was running around me and barking, nipping at my glove like she always did with the kid. I was in no mood to play. I grabbed the shovel and threw it on the rig in case I had to do some digging and I set off as fast as I could, like my life depended on it, never mind that they might have already both lost theirs.

They say it's only when people are gone that you realize just how much you care about them. Everyone around me's gone: Thomas, my folks, Faye, Bess, the kid. Like everything's over and now I just have to shut the door behind me, turn the key one last time in the lock, and leave this place, this land where everything's frozen numb in the winter and rushed in the summer. This lost land where you even forget what you were before. This land that's so harsh that only men can stand it, barely any woman would dare to make a life for herself there.

Strange that she'd want to come here after how hot Nevada was—her, that California girl, that redhead with golden skin, so sad when she stopped smiling, like some china cup that's just been chipped—but she struck me as being as strong as a rock when she wanted to be. I thought New York was crazy, but it was nothing next to Las Vegas.

That was where I saw her, with that cigarette dangling from her lips, a devilish little angel who couldn't be bothered to choose between hell and heaven. I was done traveling with this kid who didn't talk, and I'd decided that it was over: I'd buy him a one-way ticket to New York and send him off to his grandmother. After all, it couldn't be that bad, no mother could be so bad as to make all her children run away. Someone'd be looking after him and I could go back to my old life. I was ashamed to feel relieved. Bess had sent us to a restaurant to wait for her, and when she found us, she ruffled the boy's hair and he'd blushed and she asked me what I was doing there with my son.

My son. Funny how when those words came out of her mouth suddenly they felt like the truth. If it'd been decided that I had to be his father, that meant something, even if I didn't quite see what. I looked at little Thomas, who was looking at Bess and smiling for the first time since we'd left the city he was born in, and I didn't think twice before asking this woman what she was fixing to do for the next ten years.

"All a matter of what fate's got in store for me," she said, "but I'm a betting girl. I'll pay good money to find out."

FREEMAN

You can go and shoot a man in Central Park, at sundown, and nobody'll see it.

Even now I'm still scratching my head as to how she could have been the only one to catch it happening. She just walked out from the trees, an Upper East Side wife in the middle of a park it wasn't wise to wander in when you were a woman or when you were alone, especially not when anyone could see how rich you are.

The revolver was still in my hand but she wasn't one bit fazed. I wasn't keen on scaring her. I asked her to call 911, I told her I'd killed the man on the ground, but she had no need to be scared of me.

I hadn't cried since Leslie was born, but now my tears wouldn't stop. What I'd have given to be struck down there and then.

She didn't blink twice, she just asked, "Why?" She must have been a woman used to fixing messes. Little squabbles, nasty crimes—either way she'd clean it up. Which made this situation just like any other to her.

I had no secrets left to keep. I told her everything about my son lying on the ground and his mother who would never forgive me. I talked to that stranger like I'd never talked to Martha, and all the while she just listened like I was telling her old news. When I'd run out of words for just how far up shit creek I'd gotten, she walked up, took my hand, slowly pulled my fingers off of the gun. She took the weapon by the barrel, placed it in her handbag, slipped her arm into the crook of mine, like I was some senile old man, and took me into the woods. I pulled back, I said I didn't want to go, I'd be staying right here waiting for the police, but she just tugged at my arm, saying there was no point doing that—that he wouldn't be coming back to life all of a sudden.

I looked back to see his body. I didn't know why I'd done it. He might have been a criminal, but he'd been alive, he'd been in this world. He could have turned over a new leaf, he could have met the right person at the right moment, come to his senses, and decided that he'd been going down the wrong path. Even the worst men can change, and that could have been him. He'd have saved his soul, and his mother would have praised the Lord. I'd stood by my principles and acted by them, they'd never steered me wrong: the law was the backbone of my existence. But the law wouldn't be bringing back my son. Everything I had brought into this world was gone.

Maybe the Lord had seen He'd giveth too much and decided in His wisdom that it was high time He taketh away what was dearest to me. Maybe He, too, was asking me to prove my love, the love I had for Him.

Night had fallen, I had ended up at her place, a brownstone so big that my house could have fit in her living room. She told me what she wanted from me. I didn't understand the first thing about her story of a lost child off in Alaska. I figured she was off her rocker. I told her again that I wanted to turn myself in, that I needed to be judged by men before I was judged by God. She said that my wife would die of shame if she knew it was her own husband who'd killed our son, that it was better she think it was a deal gone wrong or someone with a score to settle. Our darling boy's face would stay in her memory the way it'd been since he was little.

I couldn't guess whether she was telling the truth or not. She said that the only way to fix things in the eyes of God was to help her save her grandson. It didn't make much sense, but I didn't have any sense left at that point.

I stayed with her. She put me up in her daughter's bedroom, surrounded by photos of a red-haired girl, and her teenage self smiling and glowing, and just one picture of her in front of some university, and then nothing. I reckoned that this stranger had lost someone too. I didn't ask her a thing. I just played along.

It was nice when other people called the shots. I'd never asked any favors of anyone, and I let her deal with everything as if that were normal, as if she'd always planned on hiring a retired cop with his son's blood on his hands and sending him to the farthest-away corner of this country to watch over her darling grandson. I didn't blink twice at that, I just listened carefully when she told me what I should do there, what I should say. I didn't put up any more fight than my dog would have.

I don't think a soul noticed Leslie's death. There was a brief news story on TV about a body found in Central Park, nothing more. A dead dealer—who cares? Everyone figured he had it coming: you play with fire and you get burned, that's one less scumbag on the streets now. I figured they'd track me down—I hadn't been discreet when I'd gone asking around about him—but barely anyone figured that an old man would off a dealer with a bullet to the chest. No investigation. He didn't matter, not to anyone but the two of us.

BENEDICT

I set off on the snowmachine, so sure I'd find the two of them at Thomas's house that once I got there and the door was half-open and I saw it was totally quiet and empty, I felt hopeless.

Hold out hope all you like: there's no saying it'll do you any good—that's what Bess was always telling me, and she was one to know about dashed hopes.

I sat on the first step. Going into his house wasn't something I wanted to do. It was all his fault. He'd abandoned his family, he'd abandoned Faye, he'd abandoned his own son. He wasn't a man, he was a gutless coward. If he'd just manned up, all our lives would be different now. I wouldn't be here, crying over a kid and a woman like they were the last living things on this earth.

I decided it was time to finish it off, after all, he wasn't coming back ever again. I pulled my lighter out of my pocket and I went inside to send this accursed shack and its damn ghost up in smoke. I'd always hated this house. It was sheer pride on Thomas's part: moving out of his parents' place, living under a roof of his own and never wondering if that upset anyone else. It made me jealous seeing how independent he was, how far away he'd gotten from our folks.

The only time I ever saw him get hopping mad, outside of our fights when we were teens, was with Cole. He'd gotten so confrontational with him that my father and I had to get in between the two of them. It was out of nowhere—some conversation about the traps we were going to set—and all it took to rile Thomas up was mentioning the game we were hoping to catch. He sucker punched the man in the nose, just like that. Pa was furious and told him to apologize, which he never did. He left not too long after that. But before that, Thomas had already stopped caring about anything. Can you really call someone a man who doesn't even care about his own son, though?

Thinking about that got me so mad I broke the first chair I got my hands on. I went straight for the table, there were books and a notebook on it. Some paper, that'd make a good start for the fire with some kindling. The notebook was open, I started ripping out pages, and then I recognized my brother's writing, as narrow and fancy as my mother's. I wasn't going to read a single word of his, but the date stopped me in my tracks. He'd written those pages so long ago, when we were still close. It was when he was, what, eleven? Twelve?

He was writing about when Aunt Eileen, who wasn't all there anymore by then, had snuck out of the house one nice winter morning. We'd all gone looking for her—the sawmill guys, every single man around, even Ma. We found her sitting in the snow, singing dirty songs, with her nightie pulled up to her waist, and the sight of those panties was such a shock for Thomas and me that Ma gave us each a slap across the face for staring when we shouldn't have. We couldn't stop laughing for days after.

Well, now I didn't want to burn this notebook: these words were our childhood. I'd have given every cent I had to get that long-ago time back. I flipped through a few pages before I landed on what I wasn't supposed to read. It was from spring that same year and he kept writing about the same thing, with fewer and fewer words each time. The more I turned the pages, the less I read because of the tears in my eyes. I was crying like a baby—like the baby he'd still been. I was also crying at how stupid I'd been. I hadn't seen a thing, or wanted to see a thing, now that I thought about it. I was young, I didn't understand back then.

What does a grown-up have the right to do, and what's forbidden?

I finally understood why he got panicky when winter was ending, while I was getting excited about spring coming, about getting to hunt and fish again soon. I retched as I remembered that the man had suggested taking the boy: "to make him a man," those were his exact words. And I said okay. I thought it'd be nice for him to pass down what he'd learned from my own father!

Then I couldn't help it: I was puking up what little I had in my belly. My palms were sweating. I set the notebook and the lighter on the table. And then I turned around and I saw Clifford's body. I couldn't believe I hadn't seen him when I walked in. I looked at his bloodied head, the wood chisel buried in his neck and Bess's jacket lying on the floor. I didn't even take a step back. Nothing about this day was normal. I went over, stared at his face, his open eyes looking stunned. I didn't feel anything. I'd never liked that fellow. His pants were unbuttoned and his dick was lying on the cloth like a dead fish. My stomach got queasy again. I stomped down on him with my boot, I wanted to crush him, to turn him to a pulp and push him through the floorboards so I'd never lay eyes on him ever again. But I had bigger fish to fry.

I knew I still didn't have the full story, but the one thing I knew for sure was that I was the only person left Bess and the kid could count on. Nobody else loved them enough to want to save them from all the horrible things in this world.

BESS

I didn't want to lose the kid, of course, I just wanted him out of here. If I'd been one of those Vegas magicians, I'd have covered him with a black satin sheet that came all the way to his feet, yelled, "Abracadabra!" and made him go poof. Out of Cole's sight, just like magic. I just wanted him far away when spring came and the dark thoughts started popping up again like poisonous mushrooms.

I didn't know how to explain it to him. How do you tell a child that he's prey? I was weak, I just wanted to run away. After all, that's what I knew how to do best. I hid two bags with our belongings under the pickup truck seat and grabbed the keys from Benedict's jacket. I thought the kid and I could leave in the middle of this blizzard and that, for once in my life, I'd manage to do one thing right.

But the kid wasn't stupid. He knew something was off. Grown-ups can make you believe all sorts of things, but, even for a kid, going out in weather like this didn't add up. He ended up letting go of my hand. I could feel his fingers slipping away, I groped around to catch them, but all that was left was his glove. He was gone, but not the way I'd figured on him being. He was just swallowed up by the snow instead.

Even if I could still make out the shaky light over the shed, there was no going back for me. I felt like a failure. I couldn't protect a kid, I couldn't tell his father why his brother had left without a word.

I could have stayed put, stuck in the snow like a telegraph pole, but my old instincts got the better of me. I'd spent so many years just doing one thing, moving, running away from grief, so I decided to keep moving one last time, even if it was straight into the blizzard, into this storm that just felt like a picture of my very own heart.

I reckoned I wouldn't see any of them again—not the kid, not Benedict, not old Freeman with his eyes always holding you in place so you didn't know whether to be scared or thank the Lord for putting him there.

Now that bastard Cole's behind me, with a gun in his hand. I'd been looking for trouble and it had to be Cole who finished things off for everyone else. He stepped out of the house and steered me straight to the crevasses. Of course he wasn't walking me home. Any fool could see that.

My time's running out and I have to try to soak up everything around me: the resiny smell of the trees, the sun's weak rays, even the wetness of my shoes and the sharp pain shooting through my ankle. At least I won't die in the dark, in the middle of a storm that's decided our fates. The sky's still heavy with thick clouds, but I can see gashes here and there, streaks of blue so bright I could almost cry, a blue so pure it must have just been born. Everything seems so clear, so straightforward around me, the outlines of every single thing looks like they'd been drawn carefully. I hadn't realized just how nice the view is, just how nature here outdoes anything I'd ever known.

I can hear Cole swearing behind me, muffled sounds, a "This is for your own good," which I didn't understand. All I know was that I damn well won't be shot like an animal. If I have to die, I want to look death in the face, without blinking, the way Benedict would have.

FREEMAN

At the end of February, Benedict asked if I'd come have a drink one night. That wasn't like him, so I didn't dare say no. He was glum: he'd gotten into a fight with Bess over the kid and I could see he was in a funk.

He pulled out a bottle of brandy from his father's best days and said he didn't want to waste it on Cole and Clifford, who had no appreciation for the finer things in life, who just drank moonshine these days.

I didn't have anything against the man, but I still asked him straight out how he'd met the boy's mother. I couldn't say it felt good to wrest the facts out of him when he had no idea about my intentions—but the woman had sent me here, and she wanted something in return. A photo here and there of the boy wouldn't do anymore; she wanted him in her hands. So I had to step it up. I couldn't spend the rest of my life here.

Bess was upstairs. He'd had far more to drink than I had and I guess he figured it was just between the two of us. He told me about getting to New York, about how much he'd hated the city. He'd spent all his life in that clear, cold Alaska air, and the heat of the city made it almost impossible to breathe. A good Christian would have taken that for a taste of hell, he said.

I piped up that it wasn't the weather but the people. And then I asked when he'd come. That was when I realized that his story didn't add up. A boy born in early February couldn't have been conceived at the end of August—not unless he wasn't the father. So I had the answer I'd come here for. It was no concern of mine who the boy's real dad was, but I still kept all those details tucked away in my head. The boy's first name, the fact that he barely looked like Benedict—it didn't take a career policeman to connect the dots. If Benedict was just his uncle, then the acknowledgment of paternity was a lie.

Over the next few days I grabbed a few of the boy's hairs from his wool hat, and, for Benedict, it was easy as pie to take one of his cigarette butts when he came over to the house to smoke so the kid wouldn't see him. I put both in sealed bags and folded up an envelope made out to

BENEDICT

I came out of the house. I looked at the outdoors, the sun finally coming out, the animals still a bit shy to poke their noses out of their shelters, and then the lake with its silvery color, with a few little waves on it from the wind. Everything was like before again, only nothing was the same anymore. It was beautiful but everything felt frozen numb.

Nature was out and watching, just waiting for something to happen. I had to give it what it needed, and then it'd come alive. Them's the rules, as Pa used to say. I didn't know whether to go back to Cole's for my brother's sake or to keep looking for the kid. There was nobody around to tell me what to do. I was the last man.

At the bottom of the steps, I saw footprints in the snow, and my heart started pounding when I realized that there were two sets. Men's shoeprints and, ahead of them, smaller shoeprints. Bess or the kid—I couldn't be sure which. I took the shovel off the machine, cursing myself for not thinking to bring my rifle, too, because I had no idea what I had waiting for me, let alone who had killed Clifford.

I ran as fast as I could in the snow. All this had lit a fire under me. I crossed the last thicket, where the forest ended and the land stretched out before it dropped down to the first crevasse, the deepest one around these parts. It was barely as wide as a man's chest, but Pa said it was at least forty-five feet deep. He'd warned Thomas against living beside it, especially if he was fixing to have kids one of these days. He couldn't have known. He hadn't seen a thing either. If he had, he'd have killed Cole with his bare hands.

And, right then, I saw them, although I wasn't sure what I was seeing. She didn't have her hat on and her hair was so red next to the snow and the blue sky that it was like one of those abstract paintings I'd seen in Faye's books. I really wanted to run my hands through those curls, bury my face in that hair, tell her all the things I'd never said.

She was walking and Cole was behind her. The way his elbow was crooked, I could tell what he was holding. I didn't think: I just ran straight, the snow muffling my strides. But Cole still heard me. He *was* a hunter after all.

He turned around and aimed the barrel at me, right as I'd almost caught up to him.

He lowered his rifle, smiled at me, and, nodding at Bess, said: "Let me, it's for your own good." And when I saw him smile at me, I lost it.

I hit him with the business end of the shovel. The sound of his jawbone cracking was as sharp as if I'd stepped on a dry twig. He dropped his rifle as he fell to his knees and it went off. He grabbed at my jacket and gave me a sad-dog look, like there was something he could say that would explain everything. His jaw was half dangling to the left. I swatted his hand away, I didn't want any of his blood on me.

I took two steps back. I said, "That was for my brother," and then I hit him again with all the strength I had, this time driving the shovel straight down. I wanted the blow to kill him. The bone of his jaw stuck out of what was left of his cheek, and he went limp like an old rag.

Bess stood there. She was watching me, shivering in her sweater, in the exact spot Thomas had taken me when we were little, like she was standing in for him, completing the picture, becoming my missing half.

All I ever hoped was that she'd never leave. I told her that I read Thomas's notebook, that I knew the whole story now, or just about. She didn't say a thing. The way she stayed quiet, I knew she'd figured it all out long before me.

Bess licked her windburned lips and all she did was ask me, in a voice I'd never heard before: "What about Thomas?"

I shook my head and she started sobbing like a baby.

I looked at Cole lying at my feet. He had a funny look on his face, like he wasn't all that surprised by what had happened to him. I guess men like him expect to go out with a bang, that's just how their lives are supposed to end. After Pa, he was the man who mattered most to me, the one who had taught me the most, but if he gave one brother something, he took so much from the other that it just about killed him every day.

The man wasn't dead. I could hear him groaning, choking on the blood in his throat, it was like the sound was coming from deep in his guts. I grabbed him by the collar of his jacket and dragged him to the crevasse. It was hard to believe how little his body weighed.

I set his body down along the edge and then I pushed him with my foot into the void like a heap of trash. He got stuck for a bit, like he was hanging over the edge, and then he slipped all the way in, and I could hear some echoing from his fall, but it was dull and far away.

Maybe someday they'll find him, with his jaw hanging loose and his body in pieces, but in the meantime I'd gotten justice for my brother. And now I had time to think about what I wanted to do with this life, or what was left of it.

I took Bess by the hand and told her it was time to head back to the house because there was nothing else for us to do.

FREEMAN

Cornelia kept padding around the armchair, back and forth between my legs. She wouldn't stop but to nip at the hem of my pants. I told her to knock it off. She made her way to the door, scratched at the floorboards. She must have heard something outside. That's why Benedict gave her to me. He said that I couldn't spot a bear from thirty feet and that I needed some soul watching over me. Might as well have a look outside just to be sure.

I couldn't see anything through the window, so I opened the door and Cornelia was off like a bolt. She came back not two minutes later, tugging at my pants leg, barking and zipping around again. She was all riled up about Benedict's shed.

The door wasn't shut all the way. Some animal could have holed up in there during the storm. I used my feet to clear away some snow and get the door a bit more open and before long I made out something inside. I blinked to get used to the darkness.

Benedict's pickup truck was there, half covered. That wasn't like him to do things halfway. I couldn't hear a thing apart from Cornelia yipping and spinning around like she'd found a bone. I told her not now, we weren't going for a drive, but she was barking so loud that something moved in the cabin, where the tarp had slipped off a bit. As I walked over I grabbed the handle of a spade leaning against the wall.

I tried to peek through the window but it was fogged up. I opened the door ever so carefully and saw the boy, bundled up in one of those survival blankets, with Benedict's old sheepskin jacket wrapped around his legs. He didn't look terribly brave. I asked him what he was doing there and he was panting as he said he was trying not to sleep, that he absolutely mustn't go to sleep when he's cold because then he might never wake up. That was the oddest sight I'd ever seen—a bundled-up kid rattling off things he'd definitely read in a book—and I just burst out laughing.

I lifted him up in my arms and told him he was frozen solid just like a little ice Eskimo. I took little Thomas to

Benedict's house, set him down on the couch with all the bedding I could find to help warm him up, and I started a proper fire. I asked him what he was doing in the shed when it was this cold and, before he fell asleep, he just said it was a funny story and that he wanted to wait for Bess and Benedict to come back.

So we waited for them—a good while, to be honest—but I wasn't one bit worried. I was nice and warm, sitting on this couch with the kid's head resting on my lap, the dog at my feet and the fire crackling, and I felt like the grandfather I'd never be.

BESS

Sometimes secrets get so heavy, it feels like there's no way to get rid of them without getting rid of yourself too.

I know exactly why I didn't tell Benedict a thing the first time I found the notebook. I figured a man wouldn't understand. Only a woman could know what Thomas went through every time Cole forced himself on him. And maybe I didn't want to give Benedict even more grief. He liked Cole because the man reminded him of the good old days, when his family was all together and nothing was going to change.

If he'd gone into his brother's house, he could have found the answers to all his questions, but he never wanted to set foot in there. He was so mad at Thomas that he didn't even want to look that way when we were by the lake, as if that'd spare him from thinking about his brother, but of course his brother would always be there, sitting at our table every day, popping up in his head every time he looked at the little boy with the same name. Sometimes it's the ones who are gone who take up the most space, not the ones who are there.

As matters stand, we aren't all that different, him and me: we're the last branches on the last tree. But he'd sacrificed what he'd loved for me. He'd killed for me. I don't know how to make sense of that, I'm not used to folks wanting to protect me.

He takes my hand on the way back, the snowmachine's broken down again. We left everything behind—the blood on the snow, the house open to the elements, Clifford's body, Thomas's notebook. The kid's somewhere out there, lost, no thanks to me.

Benedict keeps going without a word. I can tell his head's full of questions: he looks like he's aged overnight and I hold his hand as tight as I can. I don't want to let go of it, not before we get to the house. After that, it doesn't matter what happens.

I could end up in prison, I could be kicked out of this frozen place, but I'm sure that whenever I close my eyes I'll remember this land that brought me back to life, remember how my heart was beating even in this ice, where there was cold outside and fire inside. I've never felt so at home before, now that this chessboard has a few pieces missing, now that three pieces are good and gone.

FREEMAN

I was watching through the window while the kid was deep asleep and I saw the two of them coming. They reminded me of me and Martha way back when, apart from Benedict having blood on his jacket and the two of them looking plum tuckered.

I went and stood on the doorstep. It just about broke my heart what I was going to do to them. When they saw me, they gave me a smile like I was family, the kind you never expect to make out of a fine mess. They climbed the steps up to the porch, and Benedict grabbed my hand. He didn't grab it like a manly man in his prime, the way he did it was full of sadness and pain. He said that Cole and Clifford were dead and that the kid probably was too.

I told them that I didn't plan on shedding a single tear for either of those scum but that, when it came to the boy, there wasn't any point crying, either, because he was asleep in the living room. Benedict ran straight into the room, grabbed the boy in his arms, and hugged him tight as if he wanted to pull him into his body. Bess was sobbing and stroking the kid's head and whispering, "I'm sorry," over and over. I wouldn't say I understood everything happening right there and then, but one thing I knew for sure: that love needed no explaining. Never mind that Benedict wasn't his father: he loved the boy, and that was all a child needed to grow up, at least for a while.

Later that evening, they told me everything, and they didn't leave out a single detail. After that, I just let them be and I slipped out without their noticing, as busy as they were watching the kid, who was getting feverish. I had a decision to make, which didn't cost me as much as I'd have thought.

The next morning, at dawn, I went to Thomas's house. I had something to get and some cleanup to do. I'd seen my share of crime scenes and I knew what needed getting rid of and how.

Clifford's body wasn't easy: that pig was a heavy thing and the rigor mortis didn't help any. I managed to roll him onto a sheet I'd spread on the floor and drag him to the door. I steered the rig so it was alongside the house and dragged the sled attached to it so it was level with the steps and I pushed his corpse over into it. Nice bit of irony, that: the machine he'd sold me, figuring he was scamming me, was carrying his dead body.

I went back to the house to scrub every inch of the floorboards. I put the rocking chair back, adjusted the cushion on the seat, tidied up everything that was where it oughtn't be, gathered up Bess's belongings, the wood chisel, and the leather-bound notebook at the bottom of it all.

In Thomas's bedroom, I finally found what I was hoping for. I stuck it in the inside pocket of my jacket so as not to lose such a little thing.

On my way out, I left the door open. With the damp and the animals sure to get in, there was some chance what was left of the blood would break down to nothing.

I drove the rig over to where Benedict had said he'd gotten rid of Cole's body, and I made sure Clifford's went the same way. Only right that their bodies should rot together, in the same place. There was enough blood on the snow that I shoveled it as best I could. The animals would take care of the rest there too. I didn't know if that would be enough, but by the time someone would think to look for their bodies, nature would have covered our tracks.

I headed over to see how the kid was doing. They said he was stable and so I came back home.

I washed the sled, burned the sheet, poured myself a glass of whiskey, looked one last time at this house that had stood sturdy over my head, and then started writing. For a man who'd run this far afoul of the law, I felt oddly calm. But when all was said and done, nothing had happened: I wasn't struck by lightning, there was no divine punishment. God was watching me—that much I felt sure of now—but He hadn't said a thing, as if He had long foreseen this succession of events and as if I were exactly where I ought to be, with my strengths and my weaknesses.

I wrote to Martha that I was coming back, because she deserved the whole truth, however painful it might be for her, and I folded up a new envelope for Mrs. Berger. I reckoned its contents wouldn't please her. In it were two sealed bags with little Thomas's hair and one of his father's baby teeth. The little wooden box that tooth came from is in Benedict's bedroom now, and no living soul can say that it wasn't always there.

ACKNOWLEDGMENTS

Thanks to Béatrice Mathieu, without whom this book never would have been written.

Thanks to Jeanne Grange, who believed in *Blizzard*.

Thanks to Claire Callot for giving me my breath.

Thanks to Sophie, who cleared the way.

And thanks to Elena, Arto, Nathalie, Didier, and Andres, who showed me the best of humanity.

TRANSLATOR'S ACKNOWLEDGMENTS

Thanks to Tracy Carns and Violaine Faucon, who gave me the chance to work on this gem of a book. To Matthias Jambon-Puillet for quite a few answers about slang. To Reid Magdanz, whose wealth of knowledge as a lifelong resident of Bush Alaska was invaluable. To Jamison Stoltz, who proved to be a dream editor. To David Chesanow, Logan Hill, and Mike Richards for their careful eyes. And, of course, to Marie, through whose words I discovered my own country anew.